CATCH AS KETCHIKAN

CATCH AS KETCHIKAN

C.C. GABON

iUniverse, Inc.
New York Bloomington

iUniverse books may be ordered through booksellers or by contacting:

iUniverse
1663 Liberty Drive
Bloomington, IN 47403
www.iuniverse.com
1-800-Authors (1-800-288-4677)

ISBN: 978-1-4401-3285-8 (sc)
ISBN: 978-1-4401-3287-2 (dj)
ISBN: 978-1-4401-3286-5 (ebook)

Library of Congress Control Number: 2009924839

Printed in the United States of America

iUniverse rev. date: 03/18/09

"This book is dedicated to the one that got away and the one that I caught, you both know who you are!"

Table of Contents

CHAPTER ONE
"Let the Good Times Roll?"

As the blood splattered on my smock, I thought this must be what it felt like to be a canvas that Jackson Pollock had painted on. The conveyor belt moved the salmon at a precise pace and I learned that you have to insert the knife in the hole in their back end, and in one slice cut from there up to the head with your right hand. Then with your frozen left hand you pulled all the guts out. I entertained these endless moments by pretending I was a Mongolian Warrior at battle. Right hand, knife slash, left hand, sweeps out the insides, my knife bloodied and battle worn on the slime line. It was a great and somewhat twisted way to release the fury I had developed against my beloved for forcing me here in the first place

During my orientation I was informed not to touch my face while the fish scales were landing on it, as this would result in a nasty and unsightly rash type thing. After four long and grueling hours here at "The Mistress of The Water Cannery", I was getting the hang of it enough to make a game out of it. "Take that you evil creature" I said to myself as I was smiling a sinister smile. This put my co-workers off a bit, which was what I was going for.

After a quick and un-satisfying lunch consisting of sour

orange juice and a mushy tuna sandwich from home, I was informed that if I kept up the good work I could make it to the egg room. The egg room is where they harvested the roe, fish eggs or caviar. It was said that the temperature in there was almost tropical, about fifty degrees. On the slime line it was literally a cold day in hell everyday. Everyone else wanted to be in the "egg room", but I vowed to myself that I was not ever coming back here again. Come tomorrow I was getting a decent job even if it meant stripping at the "The Funky Penguin" our local, popular and highly un-reputable strip joint.

I just had to finish out this day first and I still had five more hours of fish gutting to go. Shit! This work gave me plenty of time to think. How the hell did I end up here? Yes, it was a man. It's always a man isn't it? How did he talk me into this?

It was only last year that I was in high school and living a simple and spiteful existence. Boys followed me around and did almost anything I asked of them. If you got on my good side you were in luck, it not then you had to watch your back.

An example of my less than angelic side surfaced when Wendy won the Art School Scholarship over me. This made me furious and I started a rumor that she had an abortion last year. After that she dropped out of school before graduation and I never saw her again. I can't imagine that she would have ever believed that I would be gutting fish in Alaska and living with a guy who sweet talked in this B movie experience.

My life changed when I laid eyes on that man who I should have recognized as trouble, on that warm August evening in Alameda

* * * * * * * * * * *

It was a very perfect summer night, in the weather sense. The kind of night when you could wear a tank top and shorts and not feel a hint of discomfort until around midnight. However it was only eight thirty on a Friday night. We had just finished a lovely meal of stroganoff, made with sautéed beef in red wine accompanied by onions and mushrooms covered in sour cream and lots of butter. My sister Effie is an amazingly fine cook. That is probably one of the other reasons she's had no trouble finding men to be used by. She was always trying to please someone.

Personally I have no desire to please anyone but myself. I decided to move in with her when I graduated from high school in June. I intended to do my best to look after her. Which is odd when I think about it, as she is the older sibling and she and I never got along that well while I was growing up? I always got the feeling that she was annoyed by me in some way. I think that she has a way of needing people and their approval, and of wanting to play the good daughter. A trait I obviously don't possess. She also has very insecure tendencies and a need to put others down to lift her own opinion of herself. I have been on the receiving end of this on more than one occasion. I have always sort of felt sorry for her. I know I should look up to my big sister but she tends to be weak and pathetic at times, and very naive for her age. Her trusting spirit low self-image wants so badly to believe people. It makes her endearing because she is often childlike.

One of the reasons I wanted to move in here with her is I don't think she should be alone. The guys she goes for never take care of her. They use her and cast her aside. She could just as well be an inflatable doll. Her list of bad choices is very long. The guy she just broke up with wouldn't leave his wife. Six months prior to that she was dating her boss at the automotive repair shop where she works. She has been engaged to be married more times than a sailor on shore leave. Effie is a wad of malleable clay

We thought it might be nice to live together for a while. I shouldn't say "we" as I sort of forced my way in, even though I am the youngest in the family and Effie is only a few years older than me.

I am the aggressive daughter, which did not set well with my parents in our strict Greek Orthodox family. While my family was Orthodox, you might say I am more unorthodox. Somehow our family's religion has never sat well with me. Until I discover some beliefs better suited to my temperament, I am stuck with the ones I grew up with. My parents thought that my rebellion was just a phase and I would grow out of it. Ha, I never will. I don't want to. I am not easy going; I don't roll with the changes. I roll over the changes to get what I want. And I wanted a place away from my parents.

Effie rented out the bottom half of what some would refer to as an arts and crafts style home in good old Alameda, California. It was a very lovely street surrounded by Victorian homes. The exterior was painted a sort of sickly mint green with brown trim and resembles some kind of ice cream sandwich. It was not all that great looking. I am pretty sure this building was old, maybe built just after the great quake of 1906, but it was beautiful inside. It contained nice sized rooms and wood floors everywhere except in the kitchen. It was charming and rather eclectic, all at once. With its white and light yellow painted walls, it was light and airy. The vinyl flooring was an ugly cream color with a brown outline of each square and little floral accents.

The top floor of the house was a separate unit and was rumored to be formerly occupied by an Oakland Raider I am not sure which one? It's said that he would throw these outrageous parties and then be so drunk himself he would take a piss on the front lawn and then pass out. I'm a little sorry I missed out on living here back then. He has since moved out and we had yet to meet the new neighbors who I knew where two guys.

Call me telepathic or horny but I can always tell when eligible men are around. That might be because I go through them like barf bags on a flight to Europe that's experiencing turbulence. I always prefer to dump a guy before he has the chance to dump me first. What can I say; it's a control issue.

On this particular evening everything seemed fine for wallowing in a nice big glass of red wine mixed with soda. I had just broken up with my boyfriend of the last two and a half months and was feeling a little down. I saw the breakup coming on my birthday in July about a month prior, when he told me he didn't like the way I ate my cheesecake. I felt that it was a sign of things to come. Crying into my wine was my second favorite thing to do after a breakup. My favorite thing is usually to find my next conquest as quickly as possible. Somehow it was not working so rapidly this time.

On the rebound I will go out trolling for some male companionship. I use my version of a net and some bait. Enough said. With Effie by my side it's easy to attract men and I don't have to do anything. She possesses a body that some people would say resembles a badly drawn cartoon. With her ungodly measurements, of a "48 DD" bra size, a 30inch waist, and bleached blonde hair. For flair she added a pair of contact lenses that gave her fake blue eye color. All of this on a five foot six inch frame. That body has got her into more bad times than good.

I pale at comparison at four feet eleven inches tall with a slender body, big bold smile and nice assets. Although I have a good figure, next to her I resemble an adolescent paperboy. I really think that body of hers; coupled with her naïve nature that believes men really cared about her is what causes her the most damage. I sort of had to watch out for her a lot.

I couldn't go out this evening because I had to start work in the morning. It was my first real job, working at the local drugstore. Hey, this was the best I could do. Just out of high school, no direction, no ambition and burning the proverbial candle at both ends.

I stared out into space as Effie came out on the steps with her own glass of expensive red wine, which was all she drank. It cost nearly four bucks a bottle.

She yawned and said "Wow, what a day. I am so glad it's over. I am going to sleep in tomorrow, so try not to make too much noise in the morning. Okay?" she said in the breathy sort of small voice that she has. I just continued to look ahead and grunted then sipped out of my glass. She cuddled up next to me on the step and we let out a sigh at the same time then looked at each other and laughed.

Just then a car drove up and parked in front of the house. It was a mint condition powder blue 1969 Ford Galaxy and this being 1981 it defiantly was an attention getter as well as a bit of a classic. The driver got out first and I would guess was in his mid twenties, wearing a business suit with had jet-black hair and a neatly trimmed mustache with dark eyes. His passenger was catlike in his movements, tall, maybe close to six feet, sleek and lanky, and not a once of fat on his frame that I could see.

"Shit, be still my beating heart," I said under my breath and into my glass. I looked closer and noticed his shoulder length reddish blonde hair was better kept than my own, and he had a pencil thin mustache that made him look suave and a little sleazy at the same time. He was dressed very casual in jeans and a tight t-shirt. I am sure he had to have a job of some sort to pay the rent, but it probably wasn't a real job. I could only speculate at the moment what occupation he held.

They approached the steps and the dark haired one arrived first. He was more handsome than I originally estimated and his mustache was a bit warmer and friendlier looking. He also looked a little more down to earth and had Effie all ready to go.

"Hello there, you must be the new neighbors?" she asked hopefully with a grin usually reserved for when chocolate was close by.

"Yes, I am Patrick and this is my roommate Braiden". The dream come true replied with silence and a similar grin. Patrick spoke directly looking at Effie. I could have just as well be a potted plant for all he cared. I could literally see the sparks come out of his eyes.

My sister giggled, actually giggled and said, "I'm Effie and that's Doris my sister. She's only living with me till she gets her act together; you know, fresh out of high school and no direction. She tends to be a little immature and wild, so my parents thought

I would be a good influence on her? Go figure?" she said with tone of voice that confused even her.

The gazelle like man creature with the reddish blonde hair followed close behind. He was graceful, captivating and seemed to move in slow motion. I thought that only happened in the movies? I spoke to him first just to get him to flash those stunning brown eyes at me. "Good evening I'm Doris, that's my older sister Effie, and you are?" I played at being sly, like I had no idea who he was.

"Oh, hi I'm Braiden" he spoke in a tired voice with which I would swear had a tone of superiority in it. He then leaned against the rail of the porch and took on the role of someone who has a very aloof personality. Effie and Patrick were deeply entranced in each other by this time.

While still looking in his eyes Effie asked "Would you guys like to have some wine with us?"

Patrick replied enthusiastically "Why yes, Bray and Doris can go get us some, can't you Braiden?" Braiden was not thrilled but answered politely

"I'll go get a glass for each of us, if you'll show me where to go?" He looked directly at me and I felt like a puppy in a pet shop going to my new owner.

"Oh yeah, I'll show you." I had been sitting all this time so he had no idea how short I actually was until I stood to escort him to the kitchen and his smile quickly turned to dismay as he followed. The minute we entered though the front door he could contain himself no longer. "Gee, you are really short, and how old are you?"

I was a little hurt by this so all I could think to say was "God stops when you achieve perfection! Also, I am nineteen." No other words were spoken again until we had found the wine and poured two glasses for them and returned to the porch. Once there I handed a glass to Patrick and then Braiden and I sat equal on the step. We chatted small meaningless babble like why I worn so many rings and I told him they each had a meaning.

"I used to have a mood ring but I stopped wearing it when one day it turned black and stayed that way. I wasn't sure if it was broken or it meant my mood had turned black permanently?" Then I laughed and asked. "So, what kind of music do you listen to? I love AC/DC. I think back in black is a fantastic album, and of course Led Zepplin and Iron Maiden are great, and it's a shame that YES just broke up. What do you think?" I asked almost out of breath.

His reply was sort of snotty. "I don't know much about those bands, I guess they are okay. I'm a Beatles fan myself; they are the best band in the history of music."

Okay, since the Beatles were low on my list of bands, I thought what else could I talk about? "Oh, I bet you were glad to hear then, that they just sentenced Mark David Chapman to twenty years?"

He jumped up and said "It should have been the death penalty." I touched his arm to calm him down and thought that I should proceed with caution to the next topic, but what?

"Did you hear about those five gay men in Los Angeles and how the CDC thinks they have this thing called AIDS? Its some immune disease and you get a deadly pneumonia from it." I was betting that he had a decent heart and he would say something compassionate about this.

"Yeah, pity that the doctors don't know that much about it yet."

I was getting a little desperate, so I blurted out "What do you think of the Fruit Fly infestation? Do you have any ideas on how to control them?" He looked like he had just swallowed one, so I moved on to a topic most men enjoy talking about, sports.

"Do you follow football? I am a big Raiders fan. I personally love football. When they won super Bowl XV, I was jumping for joy. What did you think?"

I waited for a lagging response which was a short "I am a forty-niners fan myself."

"How about Pac-man? You must like video games, everyone

likes video games!" I stated hopefully. To which he came back with a profound deepness.

"I like asteroids". His voice had a sort of agitation to it and I was thought that he was finding me extremely boring and would rather be cleaning his toenails. Even though he did not utter this out loud, I could tell he did not find me charming.

He finished his glass of wine and excused himself "I really must get some sleep, it's been fun, nice meeting you, ah? Darby?"

"No" I said "Doris". He left to go upstairs and my heart sank like a ten-carat ring in a toilet bowl after a Tequila party. I was still holding my drink perched on the step in quiet desperation while my sister cleaned Patrick's tonsils with her tongue.

This is just great, what an evening. When Patrick and Effie broke for air, I asked Patrick what the deal was with his roommate. "Is he gay?" I cautiously asked.

"No, he's not."

I sort of figured but asked anyway "Have a girlfriend?"

Patrick said "No, no girlfriend".

I then got a little more boisterous "Okay Patrick, then get him back down here please, I really want to get to know him better" at this point I lunged at Patrick's legs and grabbed on pleading for him to go get that elusive roommate of his " Please Patrick Please" I cried out as my sister watched mortified. I looked up at him with my big doe eyes and mouth down turned in a pathetic droop.

He gave in with a" Okay let go, okay I'll try to bring him back down here, but he said he was going to bed. So no guarantee okay?" Then he took off up stairs. You could hear him take two to three steps at a time and he could not move fast enough. Their upstairs window was open so we could hear everything that was being said and they thought we couldn't.

Patrick's voice carried and he spoke in a happy excited tone "It's a happening man, it's a happening, you got to get out of bed Bray, Effie's little sister is hot for you man."

Then I heard Braiden reply "Its ten thirty, leave me alone, I am in bed I want sleep."

Patrick's tone got a little more forceful. "Look Bray the sister is cute, just go hang out with her for a while so I can get closer to Effie, that's all." Reluctantly you could hear Braiden stomp around as he was pulling up his sweats while descending the stairs, with Patrick close behind. Effie was ecstatic; this meant she wouldn't be alone tonight, because I would be kept busy and she could get cozy.

Patrick and Effie stayed on the steps a little while longer while we all attempted to make happy little chit chat.

"Effie, is that short for anything?" Braiden asked to which the dull reply from my sister was "Yes, my full name is Eleftheria, it means "The Liberator." But when Doris was little she couldn't pronounce it so she started calling me Effie and it stuck." The guys both looked at me then with that "Aw how cute, she was a stupid child" look. I must admit I was again feeling that twinge of green-eyed monster jealousy rearing its head. Why did Braiden have to talk to Effie at all? So I spoke up whether what came out of my mouth was stupid or sounded slightly pathetic.

"Yeah, wasn't I adorable, she gets the great name and I get stuck with Doris which translates into meaning either the mother of sea urchins or sea nymphs? I can never remember which one. I couldn't get Pandora, Iris or Aphrodite. My parents had to go and name me a boring name, like Doris, and if that wasn't bad enough I was teased and called "Dorkis" by the most of the other children in grade school, because kids can be so cruel."

As I sipped my wine I did realized that just sounded a tad bitter and a wee bit hostile. Luckily no one was listening closely to what I was bemoaning about. Just then Patrick and Effie said good night and went upstairs and Braiden and I went to sit on the couch downstairs together. I had no clue as to what we could talk about and I got the feeling that neither did he. We sat on the couch for a long while without talking; we just sort of gazed at each other awkwardly.

Finally he said, "Look, we can talk for a while but I have to sleep and I don't know you well enough to do anything else." I tried to come up with some sort of interesting banter.

"Braiden I don't believe I have ever met a Braiden before, where did your name come from?" I asked trying to sound more sophisticated than I come across. "Well, this guy died saving my fathers life during combat in the war. And his name was Braiden. In his honor my father wanted to name one of his kids after him. My brother, being the first born was named after our grandfather. And the name was too masculine for my sister Val. So I ended up with it." "Fascinating" was all I came up with in response. "So, where do you work? Or do you work at all? Maybe you're just independently wealthy?" I was kind of hoping for the latter.

"No I am not independently wealthy; I attend college and have a few odd jobs that keep a roof over my head and food in my stomach." Okay, so not wealthy. But college means possibility of wealth, doesn't it? So I probed a little more. "So what are you going to become? What are you studying at college?" I yawned and waited for an answer, but whatever he was going to say was not going to be as interesting to me at this late hour as hi body

"Oh, I am taking business courses and some psychology. I haven't decided on a major yet, but I am thinking of politics or law." I yawned again at that and felt I had to say something.

"Oh, that's nice." Then he asked about me. But you could tell it was only his way of being polite as he wasn't the least bit interested in the response.

"Are you in college? Or do you have a job?

"What could I say except "No, I am not going to college, at this time in my life. I want to live a little and I love drawing so I intend on being a famous artist someday. The only thing I would want to go to college for would be study animals and maybe be a veterinarian. I do have to start my new job tomorrow at the drugstore, it's only part time but it will help pay for my rent and some food, until I figure out what else I want to do." We did talk for a bit longer, but then got drowsy and laid down snuggling in each other's arms on the crushed velvet couch.

Actually its not really crushed velvet it's more of a velour fabric, I would say. It was the only piece of furniture she has kept from any of her relationships so it must be special? To me it just exudes romance and charm and maybe that's why she kept it? As Braiden was dosing off I got my last few questions in.

"Do you think I'm desirable? Could you ever fall for me? Do you have a girlfriend?" My eyelids were just as heavy as his now and as I was falling off to sleep I heard a very soft voice answer.

"Yes, you're very desirable, yes, I could fall for you, and no I don't have a girlfriend and you ask way too many questions". Within a matter of moments we were asleep in each other's arms, until the sun came up that beautiful Saturday morning. From that moment on we were inseparable and Effie and Patrick were joined at the lips.

CHAPTER TWO

"The Universe Unfolds"

As the days turned conveniently into weeks, I learned a lot about Braiden and his thoughts and beliefs. His mind flows in mysterious ways. He is the teacher of things I never new existed, my guru, my Dalai Lama, my sensei, and master of the spiritual realm. I am enamored with his depth and I find myself much like a sponge that wants to absorb all of his knowledge. I wonder if I am showing my youth by hanging on his every word.

Am I being gullible by trusting that he will teach me better ways of living? Could I be heading down some sort of path that may lead to my own downfall as an independence person? I was relying on him to protect me, but I always wondered if I was the sheep and he was the executioner, or freedom? Could he merely be the sheepherder showing me the way to enlightenment?

I have all these questions, but the only way I can find the truth is to follow him blindly until the path takes me higher or leads me off a cliff like a lemming. Oh sure I believe in UFO's, I 'm a big fan, I also am a Loch Ness monster buff. I love all things wild and unexplainable. He brought into my life the whole teaching of metaphysics and the mystical.

Growing up in Walnut Creek, California I led a rather sheltered life. It was very removed from the real worlds of say

Oakland or San Francisco. Nothing gritty, nothing deep or life molding, nothing much ever really happened in Walnut Creek. Strictly middle class and full of people who believed they were living the American dream. Always under the impression they were well off, until they would actually encounter people who were really wealthy, and it would knock them off their self-built pedestals. Not too far away was a neighborhood community named Northgate, where the money flowed like the blood of a hemophiliac.

. For the most part though I lived a decent but far removed existence. The closest thing I ever got to metaphysics was a séance and a game board that promised to put you in touch with the souls in the afterlife. My friends and I attempted to make contact but mostly just got a busy signal. You could just sample a bit of the spirit world by taking a trip every now and then to Berkeley.

Braiden was a man of the world at twenty-two. After all he came from a much more sophisticated home life than I did. His mother Maxine was a chemical engineer, and still took college courses at the age of fifty-seven. His father James was a retired Navy admiral, or some such highly decorated military officer. My parents were the poor cousins of achievement as my mother grew up in a struggling family on a farm with six other siblings and never took any classes after high school. I think I recall seeing her reading a book once, but only once. My father had many jobs but his latest was as a salesman for a local alcohol distribution company. He often took trips and vacations without my mother to unwind

Braiden informed me he was very much into the metaphysical side of life and studied things of an occult nature, and otherworldly subjects. I was intrigued and wanted to learn more. Being the bright bulb I am, I browsed around the bookstore until I finally picked up a book about Albert Einstein and his theory of relativity. I did my best to understand what the book had to offer but somehow I just could find no connection to metaphysics that I was looking for. I was later informed of my error, that "Physics" and "Metaphysics" while even though sounding similar, were in fact two very different things. Physics has to do with a scientific approach to how things work and attempting to, or actually proving their facts. Motion, matter, space and time are some of the things studied and worked on. I guess people somehow come to a conclusion of what makes things the way they are.

Metaphysics on the other hand is the branch of philosophy that studies ideas transcending scientific ways of thinking. Questioning ones own existence, our relationship with other living things and our place in the known universe is a good place to start. There also is the age old question, does the known universe really exists in the first place.

This should be right up my ally being of Greek heritage and how we spawned almost all of philosophy in the first place. I thought it would be easier to grasp in nature then in books. Boy, have I got a lot to learn. I missed out on the philosophy gene. I do love the word "Otherworldly" as it just congers up a whole mess of ideas.

I had only recently met Braiden's parents and they were delighted to meet me, or at least I think they were delighted? Braiden's father looked like a spindly old professor. He was thin, dressed in a old fashioned blue suit and had short dark hair going to gray.

He looked down at me in a condescending manner and said something along the lines of "Tell me dear can you read a phone book? I feel it is my duty to inform you that Braiden gets no inheritance until after we pass on. I hope you weren't planning to date him for his money, which he has none."

I took this to mean Braiden must have brought home a lot of air-headed, idiot gold diggers. After our dinner together Braiden, his mother Maxine and I headed out for a meeting of sorts. I was informed it was a group of quantum physicists, scientists, paranormal psychologists, and spiritualists that get together and give each other aura readings and then discuss such topics as organized religions and their harmful effects.

Tonight was a discussion on ecology and how to save the planet from our own clueless ness, as well as recycling. My favorite concept was wondering if trash can theoretically be sent into another dimension. Let's say I was a tad out of my league. We did not stay for the whole four hours as Braiden and I were mentally worn out after the first forty-five minutes. We needed to cool off our minds so we decided to getting ice cream would do the trick.

After we had dropped off Maxine, we finally made it back to Braiden's apartment, which I now called home. Our tummies full of rocky road, and our brains void of any coherent thoughts, we went to bed.

The next morning was splendid and on this particularly, beautiful sunny Wednesday morning in September, we were off to visit one of Braiden's closest buddies Ralph Watkins. It was a nice walk from our abode to Ralph's, and when we arrived there it struck me as odd that the outside of Ralph's house was an even more repulsive and faded shade of green than the house we were currently living in. I let out a little "humf" under my breath at this realization.

Ralph was a collector of comic books, or should I say a connoisseur of comic books. He had amassed about twelve thousand of these fine representations of artistic literature. They took up over one third of his living room and gave his two-bedroom apartment a musty old garage smell.. He lived there with his mother who worked two jobs, while his father I was told was currently incarcerated for an undisclosed lapse of good judgment.

Ralph worked as a mechanic and was such a chain smoker that one perpetually hung from his bottom lip. Although he was a nice enough guy and pretty smart you could not tell by looking at him, he resembled someone who had survived Armageddon, or came out of the Mad Max movie, take your pick. Tall and skinny, much skinnier than Braiden if that was possible, long blonde hair pulled back into a pony tail and he wore black rimmed glasses. He might be cute if he ever shaved his scruffy looking facial hair off. I could tell he was shy and I was probably the first girl that ever made it up to his apartment. I say that because he smiled and giggled a lot while he gave me the whole tour of the place. A spacious eight hundred square feet of living space crammed with comics and other objects d' art of a dark-sides nature was the display.

I smiled and was very polite saying such things as "My, what a large collection you have, you must be very proud of it" of course he was and I think he fell in love with me at that moment as he believed I was a kindred spirit. He then asked Braiden if he could give us each a Tarot reading before we all headed to their friend Reginald's house to have lunch with him.

Braiden shrugged and said "I guess so if its alright with Doris?"

"Sure, I have never had one why not" I replied with a sort of care free attitude that one has when one is not aware of what one is getting herself into. "It might be fun" I smiled and we sat on the floor. Now this guy was only a few years older than me, I am guessing about twenty-three and I felt he must know what he is doing. He had a lot of occult looking things around his home, a few odd sculptures, a pentagram made out of wrought iron, candles, a black cape, and an honest to goodness crystal ball. I am still not too sure what the cape was actually for, but no matter here we go.

Braiden sat on the couch, lit a cigarette and reclined in a way for me to be in his sight at all times. I had studied some black magic and witchcraft but did not stay with it long enough to move up to Tarot cards. I gave up the study when one book I came across told me to renounce GOD. I may not be a devout follower of Christianity but I wasn't ready yet to renounce any entity that could be in charge whether it could be proven or not. I was set on covering my bases and not taking any chances. To me all beliefs seem to have their relevance. I don't judge others and whatever anyone wants to believe is fine by me.

There we are, on the floor and Ralph tells me to close my eyes and unbutton my shirt as I am too constricted. With that Braiden shot straight up on the couch with a look of surprise and shock that transformed his face.

"Its okay, settle down Bray I am only messing with you." Ralph let out a sly chuckle and I buttoned my shirt back up. "Okay, now that we are all relaxed lets deal these cards". As he dealt out the cards he uttered "Ah" in an understanding knowing sort of tone and "oh" in a saddened sort of voice. Apparently my cards did not look so hot. He mentioned something about a hanged man and told me to stop struggling. He dealt out a couple more cards and mumbled to himself and then made a sound like "yeeahh" followed by a "sssilth sort of sucking in saliva sound." It was a disturbing noise reminiscent of what your dentist would make as he looks into a mouth that has not had a checkup in several years.

Then all he said was "The good news is you're going to take a trip and it will be a great adventure for you. The not so good news is a male figure, I cannot make out who it is, but he is someone you are now close to or will make an impact on your heart. He will die," With that said, he stood up and said "Okay I'm ready for lunch let's go. " We got up off the floor and headed off to Reginald's house for lunch. I was understandably perplexed at what just took place and I stayed quiet all the while we walked to Reginald's.

Braiden and Ralph talked about when Ralph was going to get a better paying job and do something meaningful with his life. I walked behind them and studied the trees and noticed they were starting to change color. A little early for that I thought to myself.

Reginald's house was several blocks from Ralph's and before I could get bored we had arrived.

Reginald answered the door "Hi, I was expecting you twenty minutes ago Braiden, where have you guys been? " Reginald asked almost irritated and then he looked at me "Well hello there you must be Bray's new squeeze, Doris, what a lovely name. Come in won't you." Reginald said this politely as he gestured for me to come in. Braiden and Ralph followed close behind.

"My mother has made us sandwiches, I hope you like tuna" Reginald seemed pleased that we were having tuna.

"Oh yes that is very nice, thank you." As I entered the house on the way to the kitchen I could not help but be aware of the large cage in the living room that housed three furry creatures that resembled weasels, next to furniture that was covered in plastic. I arrived at the table and sat down, then just sort of looked around at what seemed to be a time warp of the nineteen-fifty's era.

The kitchen table seemed to be made of some sort of laminate over particleboard. I came to this conclusion as I could see a large chip had been dug out of the top. The chairs were of sparkly gray plastic and chrome. The strangest thing was his mother who wore an apron, a strand of pearls and hot pink rhinestone studded horn rimmed glasses.

Where was I really? Was I tripping on something? Wait a minute. Am I on Candid Camera? I leaned over to Braiden sitting next to me ready to ask him if he noticed the odd look to this place and before I could get anything out of my mouth he said in a whisper "Wild isn't it, just be polite and don't stare" so I kept my head down as I ate my tuna on white bread sandwich, and drank my chocolate milk.

I had to ask, "Reginald, why do you have weasels?"

"Those are not weasel's, they are ferrets! And their names are Olivia de Havilland, John Wayne, and Sir Isaac Newton."

"Ferrets, don't they eat cobras?" I said and of course Braiden spoke up "No, Ferrets don't eat Cobras, you're thinking of a Mongoose. I don't think the Mongoose actually eats the Cobra's but I am pretty sure they do kill them."

Not wanting to be left out Ralph chimed in with "I think the Mongoose really do eat the Cobra's."

So the conversation wouldn't lag I said " Oh, ferrets are the ones that are illegal in California, aren't they? Can't you get in trouble for that?" Everyone stopped eating their sandwiches for a moment and Reginald responded "Only if someone tells on you." All righty then, I let out a little nervous titter of a laugh and went back to eating my food.

Now let me describe our dear friend Reginald. Even though he was the same age as Braiden he resembled a forty-year old man. His look was somewhat of a cross between a lawyer and "Sherlock Homes." He wore a bowtie and white shirt with a brown plaid sweater vest over it,brown dress pants with a pleat in them , was growing a dark beard and a mustache. Oh, and get this he also liked to smoke a pipe, a real meerschaum pipe. Antique looking white bowl made out of some sort of material that comes out of the ocean and a wood handle where you put your mouth. The kind that you'd expect an old ship captain would smoke. I had only heard talk that such an item existed.

After our fine meal Reginald announced to us that he had received a new movie and we were all going upstairs to watch it in his room. Wow, this could not get any weirder I thought to myself. Watch a movie up in his room? This was almost unheard of. Only a few people I knew had these machines that could allow you to watch a movie and not just regular TV. I think the machine was called a "beta-max?" I think movies for these puppies cost on average of one hundred bucks a pop.

Of course Reginald was unemployed as well as living with his mother and father. At least his bedroom was not in the basement. It may have felt more comfortable if it was though. You should see this room. As I walked in behind Braiden I am sure my mouth dropped open. He had a huge king size bed, covered in a purple velvet bedspread with lots of pillows on it. Overhead was a swag lamp.

The television was the biggest you could get and this beige box sat underneath it on a shelf. I assumed it was the beta-max? No way was I going to lay on this bed with these guys so I sat on the floor on a pillow and Braiden sat down with me. As Reginald readied the movie I started to really look around and I was kind of getting creeped out when I realized every picture and poster was of Julie Andrews. There were small ones and large posters and one over his bed. The movie was none other than "Sound of Music" which he then claimed to have seen over one hundred and fifty times.I fell asleep after the first half hour of it.

From there the strangeness did not let up. I awoke to find he had started his new movie, "The Toolbox Murders" of course, what else could it possibly be? Well it could have probably been "Snuff" but this is not surprising me in the least. Now the cool thing about watching this movie was he would pause and rewind during all the great gruesome parts so that we could watch them over and over "Oh, boy" and I say this with all the sarcasm I could possibly muster.

About into the third hour I turned to Braiden with a pleading look and said in an urgent tone to my voice "Honey, I don't think lunch has agreed with me, the chocolate milk is fighting with the tuna. Being lactose intolerant and all, I think we need to go now." He at first looked at me quizzically and then said "Oh, of course, we'll just have to get you home to rest. And we will just cancel those dinner reservations at that restaurant in Jack London Square. We'd better get going then" To which we excused ourselves rather rapidly and thanked Reginald's mother "Thanks for the food Mrs. McAllister" as we ran hurriedly out the front door, and down the steps. We snickered periodically as we walked back to the reality that is earth.

Well we did get back home and jumped straight into bed. We stripped naked, had some hard, fast sex. Since we met on a hot night I was sure it would not be long until we moved our relationship to a more steamy level. It had almost been a month of just kissing and heavy petting but somehow we always just stopped short of getting it on. Which struck me as odd since we were pretty much cohabitating. It made me feel toyed with or worse yet I felt insecure about my looks.

On this particular evening we decided on Chinese food. One of our favorite spots the China House Red Door Restaurant.

We had our usual food and even more usual chatty banter and laughs. On the walk home he grabbed my hand and kissed it. We walked hand in hand until we reached the apartment.

"I am going to take a bath, it's been an exhausting day and I just want to relax and crawl into bed." I said as I grabbed my robe and fuzzy slippers and headed to the bathroom. My bath was comforting, but very utilitarian. No bubbles or scented oils, not even a rubber ducky. Just warm sudsy water and me and my thoughts.

I walked out of the bathroom and into the bedroom where I found candles burning, Barry White playing on the Hi-Fi, a pile of pillows in the middle of the floor and wouldn't you know it a pile of Braiden on top of them. I was motioned lazily to disrobe and lay down next to him.

The overall encounter was not as meaningful as I had anticipated and in fact for all the buildup it was a tad mechanical. It seemed almost pre planned, as if he had used this scenario before.

After the glow from the sex was wearing off we then lit up a doobie to keep the ride alive. Smoking a joint after being hot and sweaty not only makes you crave odd food combinations like chocolate cookies with onion dip, it's also completely conducive to relaxing your brain into wanting to discuss life, the universe and everything

"Why royals have no last names?" I think the reason is they have enough trouble remembering what regions they reside over and like to listen to the titles of these humans when they are announced. "Ladies and gentlemen, I would like to present the duchess of Glastonmykneesbury on the Hudson third stone from the left and castle of the blue wizard of Kkensingtonia, her royal highness, Rosealgriseladella, or as her friends affectionately call her "Muffy."I mean come on; a last name would be excessive.

"Bray, what are auras anyway?" I had to ask in light of the last few days and this was the first free moment I had the opportunity to do so.

"Well, it is the energy that comes off of your being. Let's

say it's a mood ring for your spirit. Depending on what kind of energy you are attracting and harboring, it becomes a different color. Have I ever told you I can read auras?"

This was news to me, here I had my very own aura reader and wasn't taking full advantage of him. "I would love for you to read my aura" I said as seriously as one can high on weed.

"Okay let me see what I come up with." He said as he wobbled a bit and started to hover over my body and trying not to touch me as his hands got closer each time, it eventually became a caress, on my all out naked body.

"I see splashes of green and a tinge of blue." Was all he said but he never did complete reading my aura as one thing conveniently led to another and well, we were at it again. After a second round of wiggle and squeak, we fired up another joint and continued our meaningful conversation.

"Do you believe in GOD, a higher power or the supreme being? And do we have anymore potato chips?" I asked with some apprehension and hope, but not wanting to hear no, to either of those questions.

"Yes, and here's the bag."

He handed it to me and I still wasn't sure if he had answered the first part. "So, did you mean yes to both of them?" I quizzically stated.

"Yes, to both of them. Their most defiantly is a higher power. But I think organized religion is a crock. You don't need to attend church to access and connect with the higher power; you don't need a middle man." Wow, I felt the same way and I was at that moment one with him and the universe all at once. Of course it could have been the weed.

"That's the main reason I don't care for the religion that was thrust upon me at birth, the whole thing is chauvinistic and the church still thinks women should be in subservient positions. They only allow male priests and you're led to believe that he is the only connection to GOD. I personally believe GOD is accessible to everyone. The only function of a church and organized religion is the social aspects. Like back in the dark ages it served the purpose of the villagers getting together. When they bonded with each other, it was a way for the higher classes to keep the lower classes in line with fear."

"You know because you always had a chain of command involved. You have the lower class workers as a really large group so the elite class had to devise a way to make the worker class feel, they were "less than" worthy to speak to GOD himself."

"GOD is everywhere and in everything like the trees and the flowers." I was talking so much I forgot Bray was even in the room. When he spoke he startled me.

"Yeah, I agree. Hey, do you think flowers can hear?" was apparently the next topic, so I felt I had to respond.

"Well not so much hear, as probably feel a vibration, and I think roses can but daisy's not so much, and I am not so sure about cactus either?" I was starting to stare at the last crumbs in the bottom of the chip bag now. "Even if plants hear the government wouldn't tell us, just like UFO's and aliens they don't want to alarm all us little humans as we would freak out and run wild in the streets."

I read this book about area fifty-one and how this object landed out in the desert there and no one knew what it was.. Of course it had to be far out in the desert, where no one could ever see it but some kind of special agents.

I saw a UFO once, well it wasn't actually unidentifiable but I knew that it was a spaceship, the thing that I wasn't able to identify was the loud buzzing sound it made as it moved past me,"

Braiden kept talking but said this all in a sort of an inaudible mumble as I was dozing off. I decided to fly over the moon and up to the stars to land on a big fluffy white cloud to sleep with the unicorns and wood nymphs that had come to meet me. "Hello little unicorns and oh hi purple squirrel and you lovely soft bunny that I am now going to lay my head down on" Then I rolled over with the last of the chip crumbs stuck to my cheek gave a big yawn, it was lights out.

CHAPTER THREE
"Birthdays Hot Pursuit."

My heart filled with joy at the prospect of another day of not working, although I still had a part time job at the local drugstore. The times when I did not have to be there were shear joy. I turned over in bed to find that Braiden had already got up and off to the docks.

He did this once or twice a week. As it was a good way to pick up cash, I am not altogether sure what he did on the docks. I have heard the term longshoreman, but never thought to ask him what it entailed as work. All that mattered was it paid well and it was legal. His father got him hooked up with the union so he would get up early head out to the dock and see if they needed an extra hand that day. If they did that meant I had the day to myself until about four o'clock and if not that meant we could spend the day together goofing off, taking a trip into the city or spending the day in bed as we often did.

I had pretty much moved upstairs into Braiden's' bedroom as his roommate Patrick had taken up residence downstairs with my sister. We hardly saw either of them anymore. They both worked regular jobs and were more responsible than Braiden or I. We did all right, we got by, and money had a way of showing up when we needed to pay the rent or by food.

I had recently attempted to cook. I never had much of a desire to be a homemaker. My sister got all the sewing and cooking skills. I on the other hand devoted my time to pleasure, mine and now Braiden's. I boiled water once on the stove and forgot about it until it started to smell and as I entered the kitchen I was mortified to find the pot had melted into an art object that resembled something from a Salvador Dali painting. I was getting better at making eggs and sausage. I decided that I would get going and make some breakfast.

As I ate my wonderfully fluffy eggs and toast I remembered that Braiden's' birthday was coming up in a week. What could I do? I thought a party would be nice, a small one with Braiden's' friends and I would get to see my sister. It could be fun.

Just at this quiet moment the front door opened, "Hey, you didn't get on today? Let's go into the city. " I said with a wad of toast in my mouth.

"Yeah, sounds great, got any eggs left for me?" Braiden stated with wide-eyed look of obvious hunger. We never did make it into the city that day. Instead we opted to watch reruns of "The Love Boat" and a few hundred cartoons while we got high. Then we'd eat again. This pretty much continued until we decided to do something really exciting like go to bed. A thought crossed my mind that maybe we were falling into a rut of sex, perpetual drug induced laziness, overeating and lack of true mentally stimulating experiences outside of the apartment. Thank goodness it was just a passing thought as I my head hit the pillow and I closed my eyes heading off into slumber land.

"Good morning birthday boy, it's time to arise and awaken on this your twenty-second birthday. It's bright and shiny and new and we don't have to be at lunch with your parents until 1pm, so lets get up, and go to "Wally's Waffle Shop! My treat!" I caught myself being a little too peppy this morning, but what the heck. It was a special occasion.

Braiden grunted, looked at me with a smirk on his face and headed his naked self off to the bathroom to take a shower. That body, that skinny, tight sleek body of his resembled a sports car ready to move when needed but also sometimes liked to stay idle and be stared at. I loved that bony ass. Some might say he was too skinny and maybe liken him to a Biafra refuge, but he was fine in my eyes.

"Wally's Waffles" was one of our favorite breakfast places and they had the best pancakes which is rather odd for a place with waffle in their name. It had a retro feel like you could even have been in someone's home that they really needed to remodel, but much busier, and cleaner.

As Braiden stared into his coffee I said "I am going to bake a cake today so we can bring it to your parents, it's only fair since they aren't going to be at your party tonight."

He turned his head slowly and with a half smile replied "So, your going to try your baking skills? Have you forgotten the boiled water incident so soon?" "Yeah, yeah right, hardy har har, I get it. But I can bake, I know I can. It must be easier than real cooking so let's stop by the store for some ingredients, please."

"Okay, I trust you can do this, besides they have cakes at the store ready made if you change your mind" after stating this he returned to staring at his coffee. The conversation took a turn into what he actually wanted for a gift for his birthday as we waited patiently for our pancakes and eggs to arrive.

"I never asked you if there was something special you wanted for your birthday? I mean I am putting this party together, but do you want a gift? Hey, I know I am going to give you a free wish, a Carte Blanc request if you will, that you can at anytime within the next year ask me for one thing, anything gift like or even a yes to something that I might say no to. How's that for something special?" I was enthusiastic in this and yeah I could deal with anything he could come up with. Just then our food arrived and his face lit up at what I had just proposed.

"Why that's a splendid idea." He said it as if he was one of those polite cartoon squirrels. For the next twenty minutes we just stuffed our faces. Then it was off to the grocery store.

Yes my cake turned out well. This was no easy feat in the kitchen we had. Our kitchen was the size of an airplane bathroom with a fridge and an oven. Oh, and lets not forget a window! I chose to make double layer chocolate cake with chocolate frosting. A boxed cake mix, and canned frosting, I decided it would not be fair to use Braiden's parents as guinea pigs. But hey I decorated it cute. I used cut up drinking straws and made a paper carousel to put on top and added frosted animal cookies to make it look playful. It was a hit over at his parent's house and although it was a little lopsided it tasted great. Which I was a bit scared of up until then.

After our quick lunch and cake Braiden's' parent's gave him his birthday gift of four tickets to the local playhouse (four so that we would invite them, I get it) we then said our goodbyes and made a hasty retreat home for a quick "roll in the hay" before we had to get ready for the party.

"Oh my God Bray!!! Wake up, wake up we overslept and its four o'clock in the afternoon, and every one is due here at six, get up, shit, get up." Nothing gets your mans attention better than a naked female jumping up and down on a bed hitting him with a pillow and freaking out about a party. He was awake now I was sure of it. I hightailed it to the bathroom to shower and start cleaning up.

He was going to the store after he picked up his friend Martin Summers, or 'Summers" as everyone called him. I did not know much about him other than Braiden told me he came from a wealthy family and was, well a bit of an eccentric character. Okay I can handle that. After all most all of Braiden's buddies were a colorful bunch so how bad could this one be? Also a guy named Oscar who just broke up with his girlfriend and I was not supposed to mention his height, oh and he had a drug habit? Okay? Will do. Wow, sounds like another winner.

Braiden dropped off Summers and then headed to the store for food, snacks and beer. My sister and Patrick were bringing other snack foods and couple of lasagnas for dinner so I did not have anything left to do except entertain "Summers" until Braiden got back.

Now let me explain how shocking this guy was to look at, forget the fact that he could have been Joey Ramone's twin brother. Put that aside and you have to focus on the tan bell bottoms, striped silk shirt and polyester vest. He stood about six feet tall and he was like most of Braiden's friends, a member of the skinny club. He seemed polite and sat in a chair while I sat on the couch and we tried to make light conversation. This was difficult to do when said someone is staring at you as if you're the last French fry on the plate. It was making me a bit uneasy.

All of the sudden he gets up moves over to me on the couch and says "I have lots of money, my family owns a steel yard and I own a house." He gets closer and puts his arm around me pulls my cheek to his lips and starts kissing me and says "Let's make Bray jealous?"

Excuse me, wait a minute. I bolt straight up off the couch and reply "Ah, hold on there buckaroo, if you haven't noticed Braiden isn't even here to make jealous, and also he regards you as a good friend so let's not ruin it."

My timing was good because just then a familiar voice shouted "Hey we're here! And we brought food." It was my sister with man in tow.

I bolted to meet them at the door. "I have never been more happy to see you in my life" I whispered in her ear as she peered over my shoulder and spoke out of the corner of her half smiling mouth "Oh look Patrick, "Summers" is here."

Pat hurried over to Summers to shake his hand and sat down on the couch with him. "How bout I'll visit with Summers here, while you two get the food together, okay" "Thanks honey that would be lovely" my sister called back to him. I got the feeling that my sister had the pleasure of meeting Summers previously.

At six o'clock the guests started to arrive. Some of them I had met before like Mitch Mitchell, who everyone for some reason called him "Biff" and no one knew why? His friend Stan and

Stan's wife Sasha, who preferred to speak in old English dialect as if they were avid fans of that era and were heavily involved in the Renaissance Pleasure Faire. Ralph and Reginald arrived together to give each other social support

After all, females could possibly be lurking about. Wouldn't you know it coming in right behind them were three females. Sandy a tall blonde, Marie a short brunette, and Angie a tall red head, I don't know why but they kind of resembled a middle class, trashy version of "Charlie's Angels".

Time stood still when a magnificent specimen of manhood came in the door. This muscle bound 5'9" Adonis with golden brown hair and wow, did I mention muscles? He had a smile that could blind a sea monkey, and a tight white tee-shirt that showed off his rippling, you guessed it, muscles.

I figured he must be lost, probably on his way to another party. It was my duty as co-host of this party to go over and offer directions and possibly comfort him if he was distraught about being in the wrong place. Perhaps he might be confused? If not perhaps I could confuse him. My thinking was a bit naughty. Oh well, no harm done as no one can read my thoughts. Right?

Just about the third time I was looking this guy up and down Braiden noticed my dumfounded look and made a beeline for the door to intercept my meeting him.

"Oscar, good to see you buddy." Braiden grabbed Oscar's hand and shook it in that cool buddy handshake kind of way. I was still heading to meet him rather, floating as it was an unreal moment as this could not be one of Brays' friends. He was dare I say, dreamy as all fucking get out. And come on with a name like "Oscar" I expected him to look like Oscar Madison from the "Odd Couple" show.

I never imagined that this wickedly sexy example of a white knight that could pull you up by one arm onto his horse would appear in my life. And this guy was supposed to have a drug habit, too?

Braiden had to make something up to make this guy less

appealing to me. I think he felt a little threatened. Drug addict? Shit who cared, I'd gladly supply the drugs to this guy for a quick F. "Oscar, you're Oscar?" I said with a half breath and probably looking like a hound dog that spotted a steak left alone on a dinner plate at an outdoor barbeque. I had not noticed but Braiden had somehow conveniently wedged his way in between me and Oscar. Damn , why couldn't he have been the one who arrived early instead of Summers?.

"Oscar this is my girlfriend Doris, now that you both have met, you can get a drink and something to eat and visit with the other guests, Biff is here and you haven't seen him in a while" Braiden took Oscar by one of his big beefy arms and sort of pushed him to the other side of the room. For some odd reason from then on I was discouraged from being alone in the same room with Foxy Fucking Oscar! Wonder why?

All in all it was a successful party and everyone said their goodbyes and left at 3am. Well not entirely everyone. Patrick, Bray, Effie and I hung out for an after party sort of party.We smoked the last joint and Pat brought out some "nose candy" of which I do not care to usually partake because it tends to make me feel as if a half of my brain is missing, and the other half becomes numb, so basically I become a dip shit. But it was a special occasion so maybe just a line or two.

"Who could go for some wine?" Braiden asked.

"Oh I could" I said and a "Me to" was from Effie. Pat offered to help get it from the kitchen. There alone, sat me and my sister who I had not heard hide nor hair from for at least three weeks. (Hide nor Hair is a funny expression don't you think? It sounds like hide as in hiding from, and hair as in if I see you I will pull out your hair, so you avoid that person.)

"Why the hell haven't' you been to see mom and dad? You ungrateful little shit" she asked. "Good to see you too Effie and how are you? " I said sarcastically.

"Come on, you know what I mean, mom and dad think you're living with me and I am covering for your sorry ass and getting tired of it. If you don't go see them they ask me questions" Effie's voice was quiet but firm and agitated. It dawned on me the parental units must be coming down hard on her for information. If they were quizzing her it meant that they were prying into her life as well. And if they were prying into her life too deeply they might find out she wasn't as perfect as she has led them to believe.

Effie has been engaged so to speak, and quite often I may add. So I am fairly sure they know she's not a virgin any longer. And having dated a married man they probably guessed she has bent some of her moral fibers. But in her own eyes she felt I was a bigger mess than her, and she saw herself as a good influence on me.

"Fine, I'll go see them, and tell them you're shacked up with a younger man" I inhaled a puff of weed held it talking through my breath.

"You little slut, he's only a year younger. You wouldn't dare, after all I have done for you" she then inhaled and held it as long as she could, finally letting out a small stream of smoke as she passed the joint back.

The guys came back in the room. "Did you miss us?" Patrick asked. "Sure" I said "Missed you like a hallucination misses harsh reality" I said, realizing the drugs were kicking in. I was surely going to feel this one in the morning.Good thing tomorrow isn't a workday.

Turned out even though it was not a workday my job called me in for some sort of review? It was ten am and I was already up even if my brain was still in bed. I got dressed and headed over to see Mr. Warren the supervisor. It was sort of odd that since I had worked here this was the first time I was called into his office. I wondered if it meant I was getting a raise.

He was already seated behind his cold looking metal desk and was on the phone "Listen, I don't care what your shipping log says, we were supposed to have three boxes of school supplies not three boxes of instant cocoa and bubble soap. I don't know how this happened but I am sending it all back and I expect you to correct the mistake." He then motioned me to sit down on a rather cheap uncomfortable chair. I glanced around this small and cramped room. It had notes all over the walls and the mandatory health and safety code posters and behind him a large one-way window that overlooked the whole store.

"Okay then, thank you for taken care of this issue. Good-Bye." He hung up the phone crossed his hands in front of him and I and not sure how he managed it but smiled condescendingly. "Now then Doris, I bet you are wondering why I called you in on your day off?"

Miffed I replied "Why yes sir, I am a little curious." He then took a deep breath made a squishy face and let it out. "Your fired...now I know it may come as a shock to you but your work habits are not up to our standards and frankly I am not all to sure you care about working here?" My jaw dropped and I just sat for a moment while my brain screamed at me to do or say something to defend your honor. "I, ah, um? I am sorry you feel that way Mr. Warren. I could try to do better. Can you see your way clear to give me another chance?"

He just shook his head, and said "No, I am afraid I cannot do that. I would like you to turn in your smock and name tag and here is your final paycheck. Please feel free to continue shopping here." I got up, shook his hand and in a foggy haze turned on my heels and walked out the door leaving my smock and my badge at the human resources office before I left the store.

How was I going to tell Braiden? What can I say? Will he be mad at me? How will I help pay the bills? I'm a loser, shit. Oh there are other jobs right? I will find one, or will I? Maybe no one will hire me because I am tainted now that I have been fired from a job? I wonder how that works. I am not the first person to be fired from a job, am I? I wandered around down First Street for a good hour. I ate a bagel and cream cheese; I bought a pair of earrings. I talked to myself like an incoherent wildebeest on the Serengeti. Is that where they are from? No matter now it was time to head back to the comfort of Braiden's arms he would know what to do. I hope.

My feet seemed extremely heavy as I navigated each front step and then up the inside stairs to our door. Was this what it felt like to be defeated? Did the world get to me so soon in my life? Have I screwed up? Oh my Gawd, I did screw up, I am a screw up. What a horrid realization. It was my fault. If I ever get another job I will do better. That's all I can do. Braiden was still sleeping so I got undressed crawled in next to him and snuggled.

"Honey, I got fired, they fired me, I don't know what I am going to do." I did however start crying and Braiden responded with a comforting "Its okay, it happens to just about everyone at least once in their lives. We'll be fine, you'll get another job, don't cry, everything will be fine." I sobbed and sniffled and wallowed in self pity while mumbling things like "life is so cruel" and "I am a good person I tried hard, they were mean." "I am so humiliated." Weep, weep, sniffle, sniffle. " I did a good job while I was there."

"There, there you just let it all out, in a few hours you'll feel better, hey, and we can go to that new restaurant you wanted to try. Right now let's just cuddle here and we don't have to do anything. You know I was fired from my first job. I was working at a bakery as a helper and you had to move these 50lb bags of flour. I dropped one right on the cooling rack where all the finished pastries were so flour , pastry and fillings were flying everywhere. They were not happy about it so they fired me. I did learn I never wanted to work in a bakery again."

He was so kind and gentle at this moment. I don't know what came over me but, I let this out. "I love you." I said it in a very soft, smiley sort of tone. Then I caught myself, oh no too late.

He got quiet. Really quiet and in a voice with a shiver to it said back. "You do? Why would you say that? Dose it mean I have to say it back? Are you expecting me to say it back in return? "He was freaking out a little bit and pulled away from my body.

"No, I don't expect anything, I am sorry if it bothered you, look I am just happy to be around you and I am grateful for what we have, if you don't' love me, that's okay with me. I don't want you to say it ever if you don't really mean it. Okay?" He was calming down but still pacing around the room now like some sort of trapped animal. It seems those words scare men more than "Hey! There's a scorpion on your back."

He sat back down on the bed and stared at the floor as he spoke. "Look, I really care about you, but I really can't handle anything serious at this time. You mean a lot to me, and I hope we can someday have that sort of relationship but not now. But I want to be with you. So please just give me some more time. Okay?"

Sure this hurt a little that he did not love me but what the heck, the sex was phenomenal. He watched out for me and he was damn fine looking. "Bray, its alright, I am not going anywhere lets just try to move past this and I wont ever say it again. I promise." He looked at me with the most serious of looks and sighed before he spoke. "Please, don't say you won't ever say it to me again, just know I don't toy around with such words." Then he crawled back into bed and into my arms, where we stayed for the next few hours until we got hungry again.

CHAPTER FOUR
Happy Dominatrix?

My absolute favorite time of the year is fall, mainly because of the leaves of orange and yellow and brown that gets crunchy and crispy under your feet. In addition to the smell of someone burning a fire in their fireplace on a cold morning as you go out to the front yard in your heavy sweater to fetch the newspaper. You anticipate the holiday season is on its way when you can eat until your pants bust a button or your zipper splits and then open tons on presents you receive that don't resemble anything you put on your list.

Ah, it's a great time of year and without a doubt Halloween is my favorite holiday. You can be whatever you want without anyone batting an eye. Unless you happen to be me and like eyes batted at you. I like to sort of shock others at any given chance. I also enjoy scarfing down so much candy that I puke until I pass out next to the jack o lantern. Good times! So, what would I be this year? What can I possibly wear that would irritate, shock, offend? It was especially important this Halloween because we were going to be at Biffs' party, and I wanted to make a lasting impression. I must wear something that will stand out, to be noticed and hopefully be unique.

Halloween parties I threw as a kid were pretty good for the

most part, bobbing for apples and telling ghost stories and eating cake after all of us trick or treated and toilet papered a house or two. As I became a teenager they got a bit wilder. The last time I was allowed to go trick or treating was when my friend and I were in high school and about fifteen years old. Carol was a tall brunette stood five feet eleven inches and was gorgeous, she dressed as wonder woman and I was a playboy bunny. We wore our outfits to school that day and were told to keep our coats on, I flashed my costume to Mr. Abrams my English teacher and received an A+ on my next report card. This came in handy because I usually forgot to do my homework, and grammar is not my strong point. We not only collected four pillowcases full of candy that year, the neighborhood housewives formed a committee and circulated a petition to ban us from ever trick or treating again. From that time on we had to go to friends parties.

What to wear? What to wear? Oh yes, I know! Let's see, where are my seven-inch platforms? I asked myself as I rifled through the closet floor.

"Honey are you almost ready? We have to be there in 20 minutes" Braiden asked as he emerged out of the bathroom tying his ascot, he was going as an undertaker, the kind you would see in an old vampire sort of movie with ghouls and creepy stuff. He was wearing this really cool top hat thing with a black scarf around it. I walked over to him and he finally stopped what he was doing long enough to pay attention to me.

"How does this look" as I adjusted my boobs into my leather studded bra and pulled up my fishnets to hook into my garter.

"Ahhhh is that what your wearing?" Braiden gulped and sort of gasped at the same time.

"You don't like it?" I said with a scrunched eye brow and pursed lips.

"Well yes, how can I not like it if we are staying here, but were going to a party, can you at least leave the spiked collar and whip home?" I of course refused as I felt it would compromise the integrity of my ensemble. He was quiet in the car all the way over to Biffs. But he had been very quiet the last few days since the whole frightening "love," incident, things were defiantly strained between us. In fact, if I did not know better I would say he was almost insecure in our relationship. Could it be he was more involved here than he wanted to be, maybe I meant more than he let on? I don't know. I do know I just wanted to let loose and unwind because the stress of trying to figure it all out hurt my head. Sure I really needed to be told he loved me and that I was all he ever wanted in life but I could wait a little longer to hear it.

When we arrived at the door (me in a full length wool coat, by the way)the living room was at least ninety eight degrees so the patrons wouldn't freeze in what were past off as costumes. Biff was wearing Knights of the Round Table attire complete with some chain mail and a helmet when he let us in. The smell of pot wafted through the air and the stereo blared of Judas Priest, "Hell bent for leather," I think it was? Others were also dressed in renaissance garb drinking out of flasks and eating legs of turkey, I kid you not. The women with their squished boobs pouring out of the tops of their maiden outfits were mesmerizing. Three people in witches costumes, ah, real ones, no pointy hats here. By the way Ralph was one of them. A guy dressed as a demon; at least I think it was a costume? An executioner with an axe thing that I am hoping was just a good replica, a gypsy palm reader, two ghoulish looking guys on leashes held by a striking devil woman with horns and a red velvet robe wearing leather pasties and a g-string, two aliens, a Frankenstein, a ghost (you knew there had to be at least one present, it's the law) a guy dressed as a fairy.

"Oscar" was dressed as Oh! My! GOD! Tarzan! His loin cloth was a vine of ivy, a leather pouch and a beer was all he was wearing, well he was carrying the beer but he could have been holding a dead snake for all I cared because his hand was not were I was looking anyway.

I looked around and said to myself this is ridiculous. I don't look any more conspicuous than the woman dressed as a Jack the Ripper hooker. So I dropped the coat and shouted "Let the good times roll" to which the response from the crowd was a collective "Hazzah!!!" and a couple of whistles. I was handed a mug of frosty ale, and Braiden's jaw dropped. The evening after that was filled with shall I dare say merriment as I met new people and made lots of friends?

Braiden sat on the couch sulking and holding a beer, chatting with his buddies on occasion for most of the night until the Swedish looking twins Olga and Inga, (those wasn't their names I was just guessing) dressed as French maids made their entrance.. They sat next to him, and were saying something in each one of his ears; it appeared to cheer him up. After a few moments they took went to some other room and he followed like a puppy. They were out of my sight for about an hour to an hour and a half but Braiden came back looking happy. I am not sure really how long he was gone, as I was not paying too much attention to anything or anyone except Tarzan at this point. We were talking and then making out like he was a hot bagel and I was room temperature cream cheese.

In-between embraces we would converse. "So Doris do you have any hopes or dreams?" Oscar asked sweetly then took a healthy swig of beer.

"Yes, Oscar , everyone has hopes and dreams. I am an artist, well, not really an artist yet. I paint and draw and I love it but Braiden doesn't think I'm very good and I should give it up." As I was replying to his query I noticed he was really listening to me talk. This was something that I don't get too often and it king of thru me off.

His tone became even more thoughtful as he spoke "Call me Oz. You know all my friends do and I believe we are past the formal introduction stage. I think art is wonderful, and I bet you're better at it than you have been told. I would love to see your works sometime. No matter what Bray ever tells you, keep a hold of your dreams. I have known him for many years and he sort of believes he is better than everyone else. In case you hadn't noticed he seems to attract friends that appear to be less than him in some way, it feeds his own ego. So don't listen to him. Why are you with him anyway?"

I was sort of at a loss at this moment for what to say and all that came out of my mouth was "I am beginning to wonder that myself." Oscar went back to kissing me on the neck and stopped again only for a brief moment to speak.

"Would you like to see the tool shed?" Oscar whispered to me in a tone of voice that could have persuaded me to eat a dead rat if he had asked me.

"Yeah, oh tool shed, oh that sounds fucking fantastic." I replied and he led me through the crowd, the loud music and the kitchen down the backstairs and to a decrepit looking shack of a building deemed as the tool shed. It was perfect for a tryst on Halloween evening at a party such as this. Being surrounded by a hatchet and chains and an assortment of eerie tools gave the encounter a sort of demented overtone but the sex was fantastic. No inhibitions, just two hot sweaty bodies banging together in the moonlight that shone through the small dirty window.

His thick golden blond hair almost glowed like a soiled halo from the dimming naked bulb that shone overhead, the kind of light that just hangs from its wiring with no fancy shade or covering of any sort. Just there in all its glory, a light burning and giving it's all because that's its purpose. Unassuming and pure in all its minimalist splendor, a light simply there and hiding nothing.

As I lay there spent of all my earthly desire, he held me only briefly. Then he reached for his leather pouch. "That was fantastic, you're fantastic, I could do that with you all night, but I have to refuel now." I am figuring he is going to pull out maybe a joint; I could go for a joint right now, sitting on the cold dusty ground of this utilitarian building.

"I'm sorry but I really need this, I could stop anytime I want really, but it just feels like the thing to do because I want to keep high right now, please don't think bad of me. Do you want to try some?" He said as he wrapped his arm with a cord and heated up a small spoon with some white granules into it. I sat there watching him shoot up and feeling queasy but I was not going to leave him all alone

"No I don't think I do, but if you have to I will stay here with you." I held him until he seemed more coherent; all the while I felt his vulnerability seem to be overtaken by a sense of what could only be described as normalcy to other people. Who would have guessed my knight in shining armor was literally riding on the white horse. I felt that we had shared a moment he would not have experienced with anyone else, two wounded humans filling a void in each other's lives that not many people could ever understand.

From that time on I would always have a twisted connection to his soul. "I am not here to judge you Oz, but why do you need to use this shit for? I think you're beautiful and I could go for you, but not like this?" he sort of had a sad look in his eyes and answered me as best as he could.

This was his truth. "I need to." Was all he said and nuzzled up into my neck until I felt I had to make it back to the party eventually? Just then the blaring of Lynard Skynard's "Trip to the moon" was coming from the house in what seemed like an all too well staged moment. I made it back into the party well before Oscar did.

Braiden was back on the couch with his head resting on the top pillow. "Bray, I'm ready to go now how about you?" I was timid in my approach of him and as I spoke he lifted his head up and opened his weary heavy eyelids.

"Yeah, sure I'm done here, just let me say goodbye to Biff and then we'll leave." I proceeded to put on my coat when a hand grabbed me by the wrist. It was Oscar and he stared me straight in the eyes.

"You don't have to leave with him. I'll get you home. In fact I'll give up drugs if you will just stay with me. Leave him."

I put my hand to his cheek for a last caress "I would like to believe you, but I can't. Give up drugs first and maybe we will see what happens." Just at that moment Braiden came up behind me wrapped his arm around my waist and led me out the door.

Needless to say we were both very quiet and did not talk on the drive back home. Truth be told, we never talked about that evening, not a mention not a word. Our lives took two weeks and lots weed to get back to normal until it was turkey time.

CHAPTER FIVE
"Turkeys are Us"

Well I had avoided it long enough. It was time for Braiden to meet my parental units and I could think of no more uncomfortable time outside of a funeral than Thanksgiving Day. Oh, boy. My parents would be pleasant because heck they were pleasant to everybody. It was when the stranger left that they would let loose on how they felt.

They could not stand Braiden. He wasn't Greek, possessed no steady income and was a bad influence on me. (Well what can I say; they were always in denial about how I really behaved, as it would look bad on them if they admitted I was the bigger threat.)

I am guessing the main reason they did not like him is they were fairly sure we were having intercourse. Shock and awe! Yes by this time we had seen a lot of each other, in clothing and out of clothing, half our time together was spent in bed, or on the floor, or the couch, or someone else' couch, or basement, front seat of the car in broad daylight in the shopping mall parking lot. Now that was a really good one and the shopping afterwards was just about every female's idea of a great day. Hey no one could tell, at least I think no one could? The time in the front seat of the car at the restaurant parking lot was a little more conspicuous because when we got out of the car to go into the restaurant the back of my skirt was tucked into my underwear, so you get the idea. We saw a lot of each other.

It could easily have been Braiden lying in the center of the table on display instead of the large overcooked dry bird. I am an idiot I should not have brought him. I mean really you're not supposed to bring a person to any family function that you have only been with a few weeks. But I being a complete moron, we were here now let's make the best of it.

"What in the hell is wrong with this turkey?" I said out loud and was ignored by the rest of the table. We chatted only minimally and in all the years I can not recall a quieter Holiday in that house. The conversations were at best forced and insincere.

Braiden would say something like "Well I guess Ronald Reagan decided to choose today the twelfth as this year's Thanksgiving day just wanting to be different than Jimmy Carter picking the thirteenth day last year. The president always gets to pick, maybe they should let the public decide. Seems we can't have it on the same day two years in a row or the American public might get bored." This was his attempt at wit.

"What are you talking about the President doesn't get to pick the date, that's stupid." I said looking at Braiden with that furrowed brow of a person who may be wrong but if I have no knowledge of it than I am right in some kind of way.

"Yes, Doris the President picks it. Everyone with half a brain knows that." Braiden said smiling and speaking in his correctional tone.

My father just shrugged while taking another bite of mom's chestnut and raisin rice stuffing and replied "Oh, is that so." Wow but we were a lively bunch. The conversation lagged as we shoveled more food in our faces. Uttering only "Pass the marshmallow yams" or the memorable "More turkey please". Shear genius.

Then mom always had some sad news about some distant family member being horridly mutilated or dying from freak accident. "Doris do you remember Uncle Demitri?" Mom asked, while passing the green beans around.

"No, mom I can't say that I do" I spoke and chomped.

"Sure you do, you met him when you were five and we took you to his farm in Turlock, anyway, he died, he was 92 years old, he took his vacation in Las Vegas staying at the hotel that had the horrible fire. He checked out February ninth a day before the fire. It was his last vacation. He didn't die in the fire, but as he was driving through the desert and on his way home he crashed his car into a coyote and suffered a heart attack. Poor thing. He had not taken a vacation in twelve years and decided to go and well I guess he should have stayed on the farm. It would have been safer."

Around the table, "Tragic" was said quietly and in unison. I could not resist and keep my mouth shut and said "Well gee mom if you recall didn't cousin Emily die at the farm a few years ago from that freak lamb shearing accident in spring? So I guess the farm may not have been any safer!" mom was glaring daggers at me and only said I was being disrespectful. Luckily Patrick and Effie were there to make things less tense.

"Mom, dad have I told you Patrick just got promoted at his legal office job, if he keeps this up he will make partner in five years." gee thanks Effie.

"How nice I guess congratulations are in order." Mom said smiling from ear to ear then "oops" back to Braiden "Braiden what is it that you do again for employment? You're some sort of dock worker? Is it steady work?" as her smile was short lived.

"Well it pays well enough, no it's not steady work but I am attending college and going for my business degree" he tried to sound like a man on the move.

"College, shouldn't you have graduated by now. Aren't' you about 30?" Mom spoke and the table held its breath.

"No ma'am, I am 21 and I am taking my time getting a degree because I work part-time to pay my own way."

I meanwhile was wondering if dessert was going to happen soon. I would like to eat some pumpkin pie before we all trip over ourselves trying to get out of this God forsaken place. The tension was going to get messier and I am sure at some point all our living arrangements were going to come to light. Luckily mom and dad adored Patrick so he kept them at bay. I bet I have room in my purse to smuggle out some pie if I wrap it in foil?

"Would anyone like some coffee? I would like some, so I am going to make a pot and get the pie ready." I bolted out of my chair and headed for the kitchen. I attacked that poor defenseless pie with a spoon because I was in desperate need and did not want to waste time looking for a fork. I overheard the conversation getting lively in the dining room.

"Patrick, Effie tells me your musically inclined?" my father was inquiring.

"Yes sir I play the bass and it happens to be in Braiden's' band, he plays guitar. He is really quite good at it, we gig about twice a month, and the band name is "The Dirty Harry's." Patrick is so pleasant when he speaks you would think he was studying for the priesthood. Dad was only semi amused at this.

My mother spoke again " Oh, well Patrick it's a good to know you have an honest occupation to go along with that musician nonsense, maybe you can get Braiden some sort of office job where you work?" I swear I could actually hear Braiden's' face become dumfounded from the kitchen. I knew he was going to speak. Shit, get me out of here.

"Well, Ma'am, I do just fine and I have no intention of working for a law firm and if you feel I am not good enough for your daughter then I am sorry, but after all it is her own choice. She is over eighteen and pretty much an adult so you have really no say in the matter. Furthermore what is it Mr. Karras does anyway? Pedal booze? And you just stay home on your ass. Your kids are grown and you have no purpose. My mother is college educated and still takes classes. Come on, you and Mr. Karras are just providing the world with bad habits. So who are you to judge me, and what I do? Besides which your husband dresses like an unsophisticated garbage man, and you perpetuate the old frumpy house wife image, come on you're not fooling anyone with that cheap dyed red hair."

Did Braiden just loose it? Oh no here comes the reply from mom. Shit, I had better get my purse.

"Listen you little snot nosed punk, you have no right to talk to me like that, in my own home? You're a guest here and it's true I do not feel you're good enough for my daughter. In fact I would not let you date our dog if I we had one. I would appreciate it if you left now and if you leave right now I promise I won't beat the crap out of you."

I then grabbed the pie, my purse and kissed my father on the cheek as he was still eating his dinner. I then grabbed Braiden told Patrick and Effie goodbye and pretty much threw Braiden out the front door ahead of me and into the car.

I must say the ride home was very quiet. I had never seen my mother behave like this before and frankly never wanted to see that again. I had a lot to think about that night. I care a lot about Braiden. He has some good qualities, weather anyone can seem to find them or not. He is kind to animals, gives money to vagrants, is smart and will probably make a fine entrepreneur someday. On the other hand he can be egotistical and rude and sort of immature.

But hey so can I. We posses similar personality traits and they were never more profound as they were at dinner tonight. He could have just let it all slide after all it was just for a couple of hours and a holiday for crying out loud.

My mother, oh shit what was her problem? Why the sudden need for "The protective mother act? The, "Your not good enough for my daughter." Mom? She was never like this before. So it must be she thinks my feelings are threatened by Braiden? Why? Bray wouldn't hurt me? I guessed it was that mom felt this guy could actually take me away somehow. That maybe she had to face the fact that if it was not Braiden then it would be some other guy to come along. I was a grown up and she could do nothing about it. She did not tolerate any disrespect towards herself or our family. Okay, so that all sort of makes sense but what am I going to do about Christmas?

CHAPTER SIX

"Christmas Rush"

A cold December day walk on a deserted beach with a horny boyfriend is just what I have always dreamt of. Whose idea was this anyway? Leaving our warm cozy bed to drive down the coast and find a secluded beach to have a carnal interlude. I was just not into this excursion. But I must admit the coastline was rather pretty in all its gloomy grayness.

I caught myself thinking back to when I was a kid. Practically the only vacations my mother and father took me on were to Santa Cruz Beach Boardwalk "Where Everybody has a Good Time" (that's there slogan.) My parents rarely took me anyplace else as I was the last child and they were worn out by the time they had me. Or I wore them out?

My father would occasionally take me out fishing or to Frontier Village in San Jose where we would pan for gold. Their slogan was "Frontier Village, That's where its happening, the Fastest Fun in the West".

My brother was off at college and my sister was at that age when she wanted to spend time with her friends and not her little sister. So, it was just me and the drag of the parental units. Dad would take Mom and I in the off season either before the tourists arrived or after they had left. That way he could rent a motel room with a kitchenette more cheaply so we would not have to spend any money on food. I would sleep on the couch, it wasn't even a hide a bed, just a couch and it smelled like old socks and a little of all the other people who slept there before me.

At the beach my mother never went into the ocean or on any rides. She would just sit on the beach under a big umbrella thumbing through magazines. Dad and I would take a walk on the pier. We even got to see a seven-foot shark once that someone had caught. It was displayed at the end of the dock and I am sure he later became one of the restaurants daily specials.

I don't know why they even felt a need to take me to the beach in the first place. They never really enjoyed it fully, except we would get one fine dinner on the last night there. The food is always better on or near water.

Food.... I wonder where Braiden and I will eat later. I think I would like a burger? As my mind came back to the reality of the present moment, I had not really been paying attention to where we were. I could peg it somewhere between Pacifica and Pescadero.

We parked and hiked down to the waterfront only taking our two blankets with us. We would leave the snacks in the car and eat lunch later.

Food has always been a priority to me. Anticipating where and what to eat next was second only to whatever pleasurable indulgence was close at hand. It is mainly because my parents were horrible cooks. My father made green chicken one night and I have no idea why it was green. It resembled something "Dr.Seuss" would have come up with.

My mother would only make a decent meal if we were having company over or it was a holiday or special occasion. I recall one especially nasty meal when my mother added flour to the mashed potatoes and salt to the powdered beverage drink mix and my father mistook brown sugar for the packaged coating you put on the pork chops. Good food was always a quest for me.

I decided to stop on the beach and remove my shoes setting my feet free to experience the wet squishy granulated sand between my toes. Okay, it felt fun. Yeah, this could be good, could be nice, I thought to myself and finally relaxed and gave in to the moment. What had I been complaining about? This was fine out here and cool and misty and damp and moist. Passing some shells and rocks along the way we stopped about three feet from a rather large gray rock covered with seaweed. We spread out one of our blanket's and laid down, locked in a kiss that shut out the rest of the world around us. Pulling the other blanket over us, our hands wandered feverishly and purposefully. As the temperature must have been about fifty degrees we decided to only remove our pants. No removal of underwear would be needed because we chose not to put any on in the first place.

His hand glided down my thigh and I felt a cool breeze come off the water with a sea salt smell and, wait, what was that other odor?-hum? Never mind, focus back on what's going on. I ignored it until it wafted around to my nose again.

"Bray" I said quietly and questionably as he kissed my chest "What's that smell?" he was busy and spoke half listening to me.

"Sea salt and wet sand that's all"

"No" I replied, "that can't be just wet sand?" As I decided he was too busy to investigate for me, I cautiously poked my head out from under the blanket to have a quick glance around. Nothing unusual, water, ocean, waves and clouds, mist, some seaweed covering that large gray rock with a tail, next to us? tail? Rock with a tail? Wait a minuet that rock has a tail!!!!

"Oh shit, oh shit, oh my GOD! Bray it's not a rock it's a sea lion, it's a dead rotting sea lion. Ooh ooh ICK!" I don't know how but as I was yelling I managed to find my pants and pull them on simultaneously. Then I ran screaming down the beach to the car, feeling an intense and urgent need for many consecutive showers.

Hardly a word was spoken for the better part of an hour. That is after Braiden yelled "Wait, wait, you gotta see it. Its only half rotted, it has to be a couple of hundred pounds, its really disgusting, come back and look".

After the shock started to wear off I got hungry, oddly enough for a fish sandwich. We were only a couple of miles from a fast food place.(I can't say which one but it has arches and they served fish sandwiches). Braiden stopped to pick up a hitchhiker. He was always doing this sort of thing and then he'd always warn me never to do it. This guy looked harmless enough, heck I could take him if an issue arose,a broken down beach bum, surfer dude type. His long blond hair was in a pony tail and he was wearing dirty jeans, a white thermal waffle style long sleeve shirt and customary sandals and backpack.

He smiled and got in the back seat. "Where ya headed?" Braiden asked politely.

" I would like to make it to the fast food place up the road about two miles. If that's doable?

Braiden laughed, "Yeah that's doable, were going there as well. I am Braiden and this is my girlfriend Doris, What's your name?" we nodded to each other and our passenger happily replied

"Sergio Drake, nice to meet you."

Braiden got all excited and said "Wait a minute, that's not a common name. Aren't you a friend of Oscars'? Oscar Rubino?"

Then Sergio got even more excited "Yeah, hey Oz how do you know Oz?"

Braiden then answered that Oscar was one of his closest buddies. And I said under my breath "Go, figure, that Oscar. He sure gets around"

At this point our guest motioned us to pull into a deserted beach parking lot and Braiden of course did it." I have got some killer weed and seeing as you're friends of Oscar I want to share some with you before we get to the food place. Because you were nice enough to pick me up" Sergio then proceeded to produce a very healthy looking example of a joint.

I must admit this shit was good, it was smooth and really easy to smoke. I had always enjoyed good weed. It was a friendly way to get high. Social and easygoing I love the mellow feel to it. You can imagine you're on a cloud or that you're the marshmallow in a S'More, or even a caterpillar sunning itself on a flower. Anything you can dream up is usually a pleasant experience with weed. Not like acid or any heavy drug.

I had a friend in high school that dropped three hits of acid at once on a Saturday and her parents had to admit her to the psych ward after she shaved her head and painted the family dog red and yellow with acrylic paints. I have stayed away from dropping altogether. Of course pot can be a problem sometimes as well, also in high school we had the great "Paraquat Poisoning Scare of 1978." Nobody I knew stopped smoking because of it. We just heard horror stories that you'd cough up blood and feel slightly ill. Nobody ever said it would kill you and hey if it wasn't going to kill you then why stop. Right?

About now my head was feeling that light hollow, emptiness and any edge I was feeling at that point sort of drifted away. Much like the driftwood I was watching on the shoreline. I got out of the car and took a stroll into the water. The waves were easy to fixate on. And I started to appreciate all the beauty of grayness in the sky and the hue of the water. Truly stunning were the seagulls as they glided over my head making those odd sounds and high- pitched noises that they do.

It was kind of nice to see them as only a couple of weeks ago I had read Jonathan Livingston Seagull at Braiden's' urging. I wanted to be a seagull at that moment so I outstretched my arms and ran around the sand making cawing sounds and forgetting where I was in life as a human.

It was very liberating until Braiden called to me from the car "Hey its cold, you want your jacket?" no I did not want my jacket I wanted to be a bird and fly off far away and eat fish, and soar above the clouds and dive into the ocean and not have to waste my time with idle earthly conversation. I wanted to be one with nature. I was feeling a little irritated by Braiden reminding me of the fact I was indeed a human being.

I was hungry so it must be time to fly back down to earth and head down the road for sustenance. The buzz must have lasted about a half an hour. By now I was beyond hungry.

We took our new buddy through the drive thru and bought about twenty bucks worth of food. As we sat in the car and scarfed out, the trippy mandatory conversation started. I have mentioned previously, after smoking pot every one can solve the earths issues and answer any and all questions that have plagued mankind for centuries. Forget scientists and scholars and professors who really need them because all you need is some good weed and you'll get any answer you ever wanted. How practical or sane the advice or answer is not the issue here.

"If French fries were a living entity what type of government rule would they come under? I mean what if they could feel and think and we were just wiping out their race?" Sergio speculated quite seriously.

Braiden being our designated spiritual leader for the day, came up with a reply. "First of all fries would probably be Buddhist and passive and second they would want us to eat them to fulfill their purpose on the earth."

I had to disagree "No, they would be fascists and we would have to eat them because they would be planning a take over of the world for domination."

To which the guys both said "Yeah, lets eat the bastards before they take over."

Sergio asked if we could drop him off at his home a couple of blocks away and we were happy to oblige, all vowing that we would hang out again sometime.

I informed Braiden that I wanted to then spend the rest of the day in the city and we noticed that the gas tank was getting low so he pulled into the first gas station we found. I hopped out and headed for the ladies room while he pumped the gas.

I tried to be quick, as the ladies rooms at gas stations make me uneasy and smell atrocious. As I was coming out of a cloud of bad odors Braiden pushed me back in and locked the door behind us.

Without saying a word held me against the wall and forcefully kissed me with his hot tongue darting into my mouth. With one hand on my left breast the other one moved down to unzip my pants and then his own. Both pairs of our pants dropped around our ankles and onto the floor. We engaged in a passionately frantic and quick quickie that felt powerful, fulfilling and disgusting at the same time

Braiden then peeked out to see if the coast was clear and then proceeded to exit the bathroom first to make sure no one was close by. He zipped up and adjusted and straightened up as he made a bee line for the car, running a hand through his now tussled hair. I composed myself as best as I could after that and with a smirk to myself said quietly "Damn". There is nothing like a hot and heavy encounter to remove the image of a rotting sea lion carcass out of your head. It gave a whole new meaning to the gas station phrase "Filler Up" although I am sure we were not the first to do so. But "Damn!!" Luckily my sense of smell went on vacation for that glorious 5 minutes.

The next morning Braiden refused to get out of bed, instead he opted to observe the one year passing of John Lennon. It affected him deeply. So we played Beatles music and lay in bed recreating that famous Yoko and John album cover. I was not as affected; I have never been a big fan of the Beatles or Mr. Lennon. I can however, see how people would be saddened and in pain by his passing. To many of us he was a symbol of peace and inspiration. I respect that. I felt the same way when my symbol of rebellion and unrest Sid Vicious died. So I get it. I understand. I also cannot resist any reason to stay in bed next to this sexy naked man. The scent of his skin is spicy and musky and when he is warm it has an irresistible appeal. His muscles are firm and his embrace is just where I want to be.

The next day December 9th was a whole other story altogether. Braiden bounded out of bed and went straight into the shower. I could not resist this temptation so I showered with him to save water. Yeah right! After getting "ahem" clean, we dressed. We decided to head in to San Francisco to hit the shops so to speak. Braiden needed to unwind and I wanted to do some shopping. Christmas was fast approaching and I wanted stuff.

"I'm ready and you can put your boots on in the car. We can get food when we get to the city, here, here have a piece of toast." Braiden shoved a piece of marmalade topped toast, into my mouth. He then proceeded to direct me forcefully out the door clutching my best boots.

"Wow, you have a lot of pep this morning." I was talking and eating and getting in the car all at once. I think this will be a good day. He had sleep, and seems to have snapped out of his blue funk. I had my toast in my mouth and had to use both hands to pull my boots up. I contorted in the front seat as my foot shot upward as I pulled the boot and my heel went straight through the interior of Braiden's' 1974 two door coupe, and stopped at the solid roof.

He looked over as he drove and laughed. Wow, he laughed? He wasn't pissed at me. How odd I thought usually he would have some sort of lecture to give me. Our first stop was one of the big name department stores, for what Braiden said would be a bit of fun.

"I am going over to the men's department for a minute. I will meet you at the fashion jewelry. Okay?" he spoke into my ear and went off to men's wear. The store was decorated in all its holiday glory and the place was packed with wall-to-wall shoppers and all that hustle and bustle crap that happens around this time of year. The screaming crying child in the toy department, the wordless version of "God bless ye merry gentlemen" over the store speakers and the couple arguing over how mush money they wish to spend on the gifts for relatives. It's splendid in the unashamed materialistic showing of greed. I also was caught up in the moment by a pair of dangling earrings I was looking at. They were shiny and sparkly and I was mesmerized but they cost a whopping forty-two dollars and that was way out of line with the twenty bucks I had on me.

Just then Braiden's' hot breath was back in my ear coming from behind me, as he now stood back to back with me. He whispered, "Take them, no one is around, just take them. Put them slowly into your pocket. I'm looking out for you. Come on baby it gets me hot to shoplift." I smirked as it gets this man hot when he puts his socks on in the morning. I glanced around out of the corners of my eyes and slid the earrings nonchalantly into my pocket and we walked out of the store totally free and clear. Braiden showed me the leather gloves he had "picked up." Luckily we had parked the car in a secluded ally way around the corner and got into the back seat. We covered up with a blanket we keep there for just such occasions and being discrete as always, engaged in about thirty-five minutes, of the sweatiest most shameful sex you could imagine. What can I say, shoplifting must have done something for him, although, I would not recommend it to others as a means of heightening any sexual act.

I admit it was a stupid thing to do, and sure I felt a little turned on myself, but I also at this point felt a little creepy and cheap, but hey what the hell. I'll get over it. Our tranquil entwinement was short lived as a male figured in a leather jacket approached us and tapped on the back window. Braiden composed himself and was going to find out what this thug wanted.

"Whatever goes on don't get out of the car." Why did this remind me of every bad slasher story I have ever heard. Braiden got out and slammed the car door.

"What can I do for you?" he asked mister creepy, who Braiden towered over by a good six inches.

"You can start by giving me your wallet that's what you can do for me. Then I'll take your girlfriend." He said this as he snickered and produced a knife with an ample enough blade on it to skin a deer.

Braiden remained calm and cool and replied "Not today!" and then proceeded to grab the arm with the blade and punch him in the face with his other hand clasped in a fist. It was a move straight from a kung-fu flick. The punch connected so forcefully with the guys face that it dropped him to the pavement and knocked him senseless for a good half a minute. Stunned Mr. Riff Raff stared at Braiden in what could only be described as a look of terror and then got up off the ground and ran down the ally way. Braiden then got into the front seat of the car and motioned me to get up front as well.

"Wow that was fucking incredible, you are fantastic, like a superhero, I can't believe it and how brave and stupid you were all at once. Man I was so scared that…" just then Braiden grabbed my shoulders with both his arms and proceeded to kiss me so hard if we had a piece of coal between us it would have become a diamond.

He released me and then spoke "I cannot believe that, it was a rush, other than when we make love, that made me feel like a man. I was mortified at first and then all I could think of was do something this guy is going to kill you both. I had to protect us. Shit it was great, I have never felt such a shot of adrenalin I want more."

Great just great I thought now he is going to want to get into fights and mess up that beautiful face of his just to feel a thrill. Or maybe he'll want to join some gang or become a special agent or a cop. Shit! As if our relationship didn't have enough twisted kinky things going for it now we had to bring in macho. He wants to be some sort of Neanderthal. Think, I have to think fast what can I come up with what idea can give him that primal feel with out him ending up in a body cast or body bag? I was bummed out now, the happy day that we had was fading away into these new unwanted feelings of panic.

"Bray, I am hungry, and its been a harried and wild day, can we go and get fritters at "The Purple Rhino?" I asked cautiously as he had this big dumb grin on his face.

"Oh, sure honey, anything you want. You want to go to Rhinos we'll go. Then maybe we can take a walk down on the wharf. Would you like that?" He was still grinning and it was a bit crazed I might add. We were off to the restaurant he had one hand on the wheel and one hand on my thigh and I picked nervously at the dry skin on my lip. It's a bad habit but a soothing one when I am distraught at any idea that causes me, well, distress. What am I going to do? What if he decides to take up boxing? Oh, parish the thought. What am I fretting about anyway, this is silly.By tomorrow morning he will have forgot all about this and he will go back to being the same non-progesterone driven mellow male I know and love. Or he will decide to spend all his spare time picking fights with drunks in bars and poking rattlesnakes with sticks. Or he could even try to become an actual vigilante and go around stopping murderers, rapists and thieves. I can imagine him single handedly saving people from burning buildings and falling objects. Yes I am aware these are all honorable things to do but I prefer a live coward. Call me shallow and silly and petty and self centered but hey that's just the way I am. I intend to stay that way if it keeps me, and my loved one from unnecessary evil. Don't get me wrong I think helping others in need is fine if there is not too much danger involved. I think most of those situations should be left to professionals who can best handle it because they are trained for it and that is what they are paid for. I would leave him if he decided to become a fireman or a cop. It's too much stress to be in love with someone who puts their life on the line every day. I commend anyone who takes on that kind of responsibility. But in this case I felt I must be the one to discourage his newfound heroic tendencies

CHAPTER SEVEN

"January in the month of Sadness"

New Years Eve had been a blast. We spent it at Biffs' house of course, only I didn't see Oscar. No one knew where he was and some speculated that his family had him put back in rehab. But no definite information was forthcoming, so at midnight as I got kisses from everyone besides my secret crush. I drank a silent toast in his honor and hoping he was safe and well wherever he may be. I also wishfully wanted to believe he was doing the same for me.

Now 1982 comes in with that "New Year Smell" like stale champagne and popped streamer smoke and gives us a whole new calendar year to play with, screw up and use to its fullest advantage. What possibilities and opportunities are heading our way? What new dreams can we expect? Will this year bring good wishes or good riddance?

"Aah, another rainy afternoon in Alameda" I said while looking down at Phileas Fogg as he came in. That was the real name of our cat, as in "Around the World in Eighty Days" which you'll often hear people mispronounce as "Finnias". Anyway, Phileas, a black and white tomcat weighing in at a healthy fifteen pounds was a quiet gentle soul and followed Braiden and I everywhere. He would go out in the evening after dinner and then come home in the morning to go to sleep like clock work at 7am as we were leaving the house.

Braiden was working steady now at a warehouse, in addition to playing the clubs with his band once a week. Right before the holidays I procured employment at a small toy shop in the local shopping mall, trying to put the whole drugstore experience behind me. This morning was wet and sloppy and luckily I would be off work about three in the afternoon so Braiden and I could go do some shopping and regular stuff and hopefully go out tonight. Lately all we did work, work and more work, hardly any fun at all. Braiden was squirreling money away for some reason he wouldn't tell me why. Could he be buying me a gift? I smiled to myself at this thought, after all Christmas hadn't been very spectacular.

Phileas proceeded into the living room heading for the couch for his after breakfast nap before his second breakfast. I grabbed my raincoat and headed out the door for work. At the store my mind was preoccupied. I felt distracted, my thoughts wandered, was I bored with this job already? It being January business was slowing down because the holidays were gone and inventory would be coming up soon. Still it was really fun working around toys. Me being the perpetual child, I love my discount and like to purchase useless cheap toys to bring home. A yo-yo or a wind up hopping little chicken would make up for the low pay and lack of any advancement in this place. I knew it was not where I was going to work for the rest of my life. It was just another interim job until I could locate something to do that would provide more mental stimulation and a better paycheck.

I just haven't found my calling yet and somebody has to work in retail. Retail does have many an advantage, don't get me wrong. I love stores, I like helping others spend their money and face it, humans are much like pack rats and like to own lots of really useless stuff. We only need food, shelter and some clothing to cover our bodies. Anything else is just to fill the empty spaces of our own insecure little egos. Today though I was really happy to get out of there and think seriously of what I want to actually do with my life. The walk home from work was dreary and had a chilly breeze to it. There were faint smells of cookies and fires in fireplaces coming out of some of the houses as I walked by. I dragged my feet a little kicking rocks as I went along and for a minute there I felt like I did as a kid walking home after school. I wished I had some one to play with, I thought to myself and grinned, wonder if Oscar was home? I was going right by his house. Yeah that was an evil little thought. I kept walking and sped up deciding it would be best just to get home.

Later that night after dinner Braiden and I decided to take one of our long walks around the block. Who cares if it was raining, it was clean air and dare I say almost romantic. We walked out and so did Phileas right behind us. We headed down the street and so did Phileas, right behind us. We turned the corner and of course the cat did as well. He followed us all around the block, getting rained on but was hardly bothered by it. He is really quite cute and he would run a little and then stop and smell something and then run some more to catch up with us. I decided it was time to discuss my future with Braiden at this point, the walk outdoors was invigorating and crisp and I was relaxed enough to just run some ideas before him. Sometimes he could be less than supportive of my plans but tonight I didn't care I just felt like I needed some clarity.

"Honey" I said cautiously then continued "I think come spring I may want to take some college courses. What do you think?" he was actually sounded happy in his reply.

"I think that's a great idea, I love taking courses there myself. Maybe you and I could take something together since you have never attended there before. It would make it easier and more fun to get you started. I would be willing to help with your tuition a little. Have you got any ideas on what you want to study? I remember you talking of working with animals or how about some psych classes?"

Wow, my heart was light and happy and I was feeling that

this could be a good decision. "Ah, I haven't' thought that far? I like your suggestions on what you think I would be good at, but I was thinking of some sort of art degree?" I was just glad he seemed excited by the prospect of me being a college enrollee.

"Well, art degrees aren't lucrative and honey your art isn't special enough to get you noticed at this point. I think you could do well with data processing or computers, but taking some simple business courses would be really helpful. No matter what you pursue, you'll always need a good knowledge of how to run a company. But we can look into some courses tomorrow if you like?" I agreed. We made it back home and up the stairs, and as we went inside Phileas rubbed against Braiden's pants leg and then wandered off into the evening. I suppose he had enough of us.

The next morning I went to the door at 7am and even though it was not a work morning I wanted to be sure to let the cat in. But he wasn't there. "That's odd?" I thought to myself. Maybe he was just late. So I had breakfast and then went to the door again. It was now about eight thirty and still no sign of Phileas? By the time Braiden made it home that afternoon I was frantic. Our beloved cat had not made it home and I wanted to go to the animal shelters and look for him. I had already been around the neighborhood a few times. I even knocked on neighbor's doors for assistance and asked everyone I could find if they had seen him. Although our neighbors are very nice and pleasant it turned up nothing.

The first local animal shelter we arrived at said they admitted a black and white cat early this morning and we were led to where he was. I saw him and broke down in tears. He cried out to us but could not stand up on his back legs. We were informed that he was hit by a car and to save him he needed surgery. The cost would be two hundred dollars but there were no guarantees that he would recover completely. The results would be uncertain. My stomach felt queasy my heart sank and I wanted to throw up. I ran out to the car crying, leaving Braiden to make the horrible and heart wrenching decision to let them put our cat to sleep. No longer would he follow us around the block as we took our walk. No more cuddling on the couch on a cold morning or sharing my tuna with him. I love all animals, all kinds of dogs and cats and birds and other creatures. I have had many pets in my day. But there was something sweet and special about this gentle soul. I will miss him forever. The world always becomes a little drearier when any animal passes away. They bring joy and companionship, unconditional love and peace and comfort to our lives when no one else bothers to do so.

When we arrived back home I just sat on the couch staring at Phileas's little mouse toy that he played with when he wasn't napping. I did not feel like eating, or going out, or getting high. I didn't even feel like having sex. My mourning seemed to take all my emotional energy. I just felt like going to bed and I think Braiden felt the same way because that's what we did. We just curled up in bed and fell into a deep melancholy slumber. Maybe tomorrow life would look better. As for tonight it was just a dark night.

Morning came around and we were still very sad however that sadness was eclipsed by an intense hunger as we went to bed at 7:30pm last night without eating. Now we were ravenous, sad and ravenous. So its time once again to head to "Wally's" and pig out on every item listed on the menu until we burst. Yes that's a good plan. Phileas would have wanted us to gorge ourselves. He was a joyful being who took pleasure in simple things.

As I shoved the fourth bite of egg and pancake into my mouth I spoke "Bray I think we should go talk to your counselor buddies at the collage and then go into San Francisco today, we need to get out. I need to get out, especially after yesterday's bummer events"

"Yes, I think so too, lets go to Steinhart after the college, that's where Phileas would want us to go, don't you think? " he said smiling from ear to ear. Steinhart is our aquarium in San Francisco, so it seemed most appropriate.

We made it over to the college at about ten in the morning. It was a great time to meet some of Braiden's school buddies, teachers as well as some counselors he knew. He gave me a grand tour. First we saw the audio-visual room where he helped out by repairing TV's , recorders, projectors and sound equipment that classrooms use as teaching aids. They check them out and he would deliver them. He actually got paid for doing this, a cushy gig at that. After that we met Steve and Sandy who also helped him out in there. We went over to the art department and met the instructor there, Mrs. Wolfgrade. She was also a photographer who studied under the famous Ansel Adams for a while. She was cool and I would love to take a class under her.

We went to meet Mrs. Smith one of the counselors there who adored Braiden and was happy to meet me and answered any questions I had. I was comfortable just walking around and taking in all the activity the school had to offer.

I could do it. I could be a student. Braiden must have said hello to about seventy-five people before we completed our journey and headed off to San Francisco, he obviously was very popular. It's that charming persona of his. A hybrid of , "The Fonz" from "Happy Days" and "Eddie Haskal" from "Leave it to Beaver".

Steinhart Aquarium is a wonderful magical place full of sea creatures located in Golden Gate park in San Francisco where there is also the Japanese Tea Garden across the street which I love, and of course the Museum of Art. It's a wonderful way to spend a day, especially during the week when it's not crowded.

The only visitors they would have besides us today were the scores of kids there on school field trips. Kids are great in an aquarium, lots of "Ooos" and "Ahhhs" could be heard as they point and become easily enamored with the colorful fish and aquatic life. They remained rather well behaved in there. Braiden and I stopped in front on the salmon exhibit, God only knows why. I think they are a rather unattractive fish. I never cared for their taste much, either. I am more of a Piranha aficionado, not to eat them just to look at them and imagine how they eat their prey, being one of the most terrifying and deadly fish on the planet. I am sure some people probably eat them because face it, for every bizarre thing on earth there is a human somewhere that has eaten it.

I also love the colorful little clown fish and all those cute jellyfish. Some species are deadly but they are still really cute. Other fish were interesting but the Salmon we had stopped in front of were definitely not cute.

"Sweetie, how do you feel about Salmon?" Braiden asked while making fish faces at the tank.

"How am I supposed to feel about them? They're alright I guess. Why do you ask?"

"No reason, just that I have a brother who lives up in Ketchikan Alaska and gets on a fishing boat once or twice each summer season. I have wanted to go there the last couple of years .Do you think you'd want to go with me?" He said this while still staring into the tank.

"Are you out of your freaking mind?" I had to say freaking as we were flanked by small children. I spoke quietly but still received disapproving looks from some of the teachers and adults chaperoning the kids. I went into a sort of shock when I realized he wasn't kidding at all. "Bray, you really want to go to Alaska? It's really cold there and it snows and you know what happens in extreme snow, people eat each other. That's what those settlers crossing through that mountain passage did. There's wilderness and there has to be a bunch of undesirables up there. I have heard rumors that convicts and people who commit crimes go up there to hide out because they can never be found! It just sounds like a nightmare to me. But if you want to go be my guest."

"No, I won't go unless you come with me to share the experience. Forget it, forget I brought it up, so let's just head over to the tea garden." He sounded disappointed, but hell no, I won't go. You're not getting me up to the great white north. Shit, I don't even go to Tahoe when it's snowing, because, as I have already explained, I know I would be the first one on the menu. He grabbed me by the hand and we walked on over to the tea garden. A splendid serene place full of flowers and trees and bridges to walk over and then you get to sit at a little table and have tea and cookies. This was my kind of place. Not like I would imagine Alaska would be. Why the hell would anyone want to go to Alaska?

Braiden snapped his finger and said," I just remembered. You told me for my birthday I could have any wish within reason granted. I want to use my wish and take you to Alaska.

"Whoa, let me think about that for awhile." Was that wish within reason? We will see.

The days progressed and there was little talk of the great white north, although I could feel Braiden had not fully given up on the subject. Today I just wasn't in the mood to bring it up and discuss it. That would have to wait until tomorrow, because today I was happy. I was seeing a friend of mine from high school by the name of "Sparky." His real name's Sammie Smith but all of his buddies call him "Sparky". I adore this guy, he is creative like me, but much more easy going and warm and friendly not like me. We tried to be more than friends but I just wasn't his type. Not sure if it was my height? It tends to put a lot of guys off. In my world though everyone is taller than me anyway so I just learn to live with it. Tall women really can't stand me when I end up with a tall guy because they feel it's some sort of line I am crossing. I say piss on them. As I tell a lot of people when they remark about height, "it makes no difference when you're lying down". Or it could be because I have hazel eyes and he prefers blue? I don't know, I never really asked him. But we remained friends and that means a lot to me. I find him fun and fascinating. I have not seen him since we graduated months ago.

He is flying in from visiting his mother in Ohio, and I get to pick him up at the Oakland airport and drive him home to Pleasant Hills. It's a city right next to Walnut Creek, California where I was raised. Alameda to the Oakland airport is a short trip but Oakland to Pleasant Hills takes about forty-five minutes or so. The terminal where I was to pick him up was crowded for some reason but there I saw him from twenty-feet away coming towards me a big mop of curly black hair and warm smile from ear to ear, peaking out from his artistically maintained goatee.

"Hey, handsome," I yelled and ran with arms outstretched. "Hey, it's good to see you too." He put his luggage down and proceeded to hug me so tight that I could feel he sincerely was happy to see me. We wondered through the terminal to the car with minimal chitchat. We just wanted to get out of the noisy crowded place.

"Whose car is this?" he looked a bit shocked when he said it.

"Oh, this is Brays' car. I get to borrow it today, mine is in the shop. We are going to stop by our place so you can meet him, and so I can use the bathroom before I drive you home. Okay? I really want you to meet him. I have met most of his friends and he hasn't met any of mine."

"Yeah that would be fine." Sparky's voice has a low and gentle tone to it that was also sort of dreamy and hypnotic.

"We'll be here for a few minutes. Make yourself at home while I get a drink of water and use the can." I am such a lady when I speak sometimes. Sparky sat down in the living room on the couch and after a minute or so, Braiden walked in from the bedroom.

"Doris is that you? Oh, hello? You must be "Spud's"?" Braiden extended his hand to offer a half-hearted greeting. Then continued "Don't get up."

To which the reply was a correctional "Hi, no it's not "Spud's" it's "Sparky" but you can call me Sam. And you must be Brandon?"

"No it's Braiden, but you can call me Braiden. So, you went to high school with Doris. Do you have any juicy details to tell me about her? Was she a slut?" Braiden asked only half jokingly. Sparky's jaw must have dropped a little, as he came to my defense.

"Ah, I beg your pardon? No she was not, nor is she a slut. She's a good person and talented, have you seen her artwork?"

Braiden replied, "Yeah I've seen her artwork and between you and me it's not very good. She wouldn't make it as an artist, I try not to encourage her or get her hopes up about her art I think she should learn about business instead." It's a small place we live in and I heard every word while I was in the bathroom. I came out at this point with a plastered smile and shook off the disappointment that hung over me. After all I was going to spend time with "Sparky" someone who just demonstrated he was even more of a dear friend than I thought.

"Hi honey" I said as I kissed Braiden. "You ready to head out Sparky?" After Braiden and Sparky glared at each we got in the car and headed out on the highway. Sparky was uncharacteristically quiet for quite a while, so I spoke.

"So, you never said how your mother is? Was it a good visit? Nice plane ride? Did they feed you on the plane? We could stop for a bite to eat if you like?"

Sparky looked straight ahead all he said was "My mothers fine, okay visit, too much turbulence on the plane, no food, yes I would like a burger and Braiden is an asshole why are you with him?" I somehow knew this was going to come up. Just not so soon in our visit.

"Look he does care about me, doesn't want me to get my feelings hurt that's why he is honest in his response to my artwork or if I am not doing something very well. He is in college and he is a bit older than me. He has some good qualities. Have you heard from any of the old gang lately" We stopped the car and went into Plaza Burgers for some food.

"Now that you mention it Sherry called me a few weeks ago and told me that Wendy, the quiet chick in your Art Class killed herself. It turned out that the rumor you started was true and her father abused her."

"What a waste of a good Art Scholarship. Now let's get back to talking about my problems, specifically, how do I handle Braiden?"

Sparky was a little mad "Yeah, he doesn't want anyone else to hurt your feelings so he can do it exclusively, he's an ass, and probably a little sadistic." We pretty much ate our food in silence. What could I say to that last remark? I was starting to wonder why a lot of people didn't like Braiden when they met him.

As I dropped my dear friend at his house and walked him to the door with his luggage, we said our good byes.

"He wants me to go to Alaska with him this spring." I sort of mumbled this as he hugged me.

He just pulled away shook his head and with a little smirk said "Let me know how that turns out." Then he turned and entered the door.

I drove back home without even turning on the radio. I wanted silence to think and some times the car and an ample drive can provide just the right atmosphere to sort stuff out. I loved Braiden, even though I did make that vow never to bring it up again. He cared about me, I was sure of it. At this point in our lives he wasn't fully supportive of my wants and dreams and that was a little troubling. Yes he could be insulting, but I could forgive him that because I felt he really did it out of the sincere intentions of sparing my feelings of deeper hurt. Was I just trying to justify this relationship? Maybe it was going nowhere? Maybe he was a bad influence on me? I could be just too young for him. He was smart and knew more about living than I did. Or so it seems. Still, I could not overlook this weird negative response to him by people who I believed loved me.\

How would I do in Alaska with him? He really wants to go, but what about me? Would I perish in a freak accident? It is also possible that a bear may eat me? How would I survive in the wild? Probably better than I am surviving here in the so called civilized world. Let's face it my track record has not been exemplary. I suppose I could screw up just as badly here as there. The thing is, did I want to find out? Was I ready to find my proverbial balls and brave it? I would have to give it more thought. I would not mention anything to Braiden until I knew for sure what I wanted to do. Well by this time my ride was over and I pulled into the safety of the driveway.

CHAPTER EIGHT

"Pop goes the Weasel Cause the Weasel Goes POP!"

"Buzzzzzzzz, Buzzzzzz" it was that warm and familiar sound of our door bell, the main one, downstairs. Who could it be? I wondered as I was the only one home today and it was lunchtime. I headed down the stairs happily with a spring in my step until I saw through the glass part of the door. "Gulp" it was my father, and one of his worker buddies Barry. Then it got worse, I realized if I could see them…they could see me, and coming from upstairs, where I was not supposed to be if I was in fact living with my sister. "Shit"

Effie ratted me out! So my Pop has popped by to visit. Now wait minute, I may be jumping to conclusions. Maybe he just wanted to visit. He never wants to visit and especially after our little turkey day mishap and then Christmas going the way it did, that whole scene with my mother throwing presents and Braiden dumping the tray of cookies and then jumping up and down on them. It was rather ugly and childish but amusing to say the least. I would have imagined he wanted to stay clear of Braiden.

Okay, so why am I shaking, look I am nineteen. Come on,

my parents have no real say in what I do. So what if I am living in sin with an older man. It's nobodies business but my own, right? But maybe I should have been honest about it? It's a little late to ponder that now.

As I swung open the door I placed a big smile on my face and a happy "Hi Dad, Barry, nice to see you what brings you by here?" Dad and Barry were dressed in their expensive suits so it meant that they had to go into the main office. Usually the dress code was casual, a collar shirt and slacks as they made their rounds. Barry was a large man, very round and wore glasses, also both his front teeth were missing, I don't know how, no one ever told me and I did not ask. He usually kept a partial in his mouth to cover the space up but sometimes only put it in to eat. He has a rather sunny disposition and laughs easily and loudly. My mother has never enjoyed his company because she thinks he is uncouth and unrefined. Yeah, right, this coming from a woman who probably wouldn't have thought twice about snapping the neck of a rabbit for family dinner. Anyway they looked nice today.

" Barry and I got out of our meeting in Oakland early and thought we'd come by and take you to lunch." he paused, looked around past me as if to see whether I was home alone, then continued with "Why were you upstairs?" I knew it was coming but could I come up with a viable answer? I am pretty sure he knew I was shacking up with Braiden. And he knew that I knew he knew? Anyway, think?

Why was I up there? Ah, this'll work "Braiden is out of town and I said I would go water his plants for him." Yeah, whew, that was close.

"Oh, I figured it was something like that" he replied with that tone of voice that says I don't believe you but I really don't want to know the truth.

Well, looks like dad got a brand new Lincoln Continental. American luxury cars were the only type of car my mother let him buy. She would say that all the rich and sophisticated people owned them and that when she was a child on the farm they would get a visit from Uncle Andreas who came direct from the old country and worked and lived in the city as a contractor in the cement business. He made an unheard of amount of money compared to her family. I can only guess what all the cement was really being used for. I speculate he was really into "water proof shoes" if you catch my drift. This one was nicer than the ones he usually purchased .It had a dark blue exterior and cream leather interior only about a year old, and must have set him back a bundle as it was the largest model they make. The only car larger would be a limousine. It has to be for the benefit of mother as dad did travel out of town on business a lot.

There's a cliché' that married men buy their wives nice new cars when they've been caught cheating! Hey! Wait a minute? No, not my father? That would be ridiculous? Wouldn't it? An affair? It finally dawned on me, yeah it was possible, dad you sly old dog. That would explain a lot of shit. It all made sense. Playing on his car cassette deck was what else Maria Muldaur, and "midnight at the oasis." My father loves this song about camels and sand dunes it's a little corny for my taste at least it brought his listening tastes into the twentieth century. He used to listen to big band music and liked Doris Day can you believe it. Hey! Maybe I can tell people I was named after her?

Anyway, off we went to The Four Dragons restaurant, for a much-earned lunch, after the little performance I put on at the door. Did dad really know? I get the feeling he did. For whatever reason though he never came out and asked me. I think he just missed having me around and wanted to visit. Oh, that's weird. He never visited with many of our relatives. Sure he would visit with his brother's when he got a chance. But usually didn't visit me or Effie, and our brother is a freelance photographer and has been working in Europe for the last year and a half but would probably come home to live with mom and dad again soon. He has already done this on several occasions. Effie and Patrick would have the occasional Sunday dinner with them, but not much more.

Then there was our uncle Stephan,, Dads favorite brother, who was married and had three kids and never came to visit, so yeah, ·maybe dad was lonely? I don't know why but having lunch here with Barry and Dad I felt like I was about six years old. Maybe I should ask the waiter for a booster seat? When I was a small child, dad would take me to work with him sometimes, and on his route the store and deli owners would feed me all day while he was filling his orders. It was great .I would be led into the back room, warehouse or office and fed doughnuts and pastries. Sandwiches and sodas and all the candy I would want. Just because I was Elias Karras' little kid, everybody was Dad's friend. His clients on his route loved him and I could have anything I wanted. Of course I would get home that night with a stomachache. It was so bad sometimes I was a pale shade of green for days after words. During the summer I got to go on his route at least one time a week.

So, here we were at one of the finest Chinese restaurants in Oakland eating fried rice and moo-shoo pork and egg rolls. I got my favorite soup, war-won ton which is made with more vegetables and whole baby squids added to it. I like to eat them with the little tentacles just dangling out of my mouth. As I chew repeatedly on their rubbery bodies it makes me feel as if I am some sort of giant, I imagine I am wading through the ocean and actually eating squids that are sixty-feet long.

"Dad I have decided I would like to take some college courses, maybe business or art? I haven't decided which, yet. I think I'll attend in the spring or fall?" I spoke as I leaned forward and slurped while swinging my legs back and forth under my chair. The next few spoonfuls had some of my hair in alongside with the squid.

My father sounded skeptical and amazed at the same time, not an easy emotional combination to convey I might add. "Wow, that's, that's remarkable! I am really happy to hear this. Barry did hear what my daughter just said?"

"Yes Eli, that's great, and you were afraid she was pissing her life away." He spoke and laughed a little. Troublesome thing is dad laughed as well. They were pleased to hear this but it made me feel a little like I was the punch line. Oh well it's still better than having him think of me as a problem child. Maybe now I would get some respect. I slurped some more soup and found another squid. Oh, boy I thought I had eaten them all. Come here you succulent little treasure.

"Maybe now you'll meet some nice young college boys your own age? Maybe even a guy that will make something of his life. I will have your mother make up your old room for you to move home, she will be thrilled to hear this.Of course you are moving home? Right?" I felt a tentacle stick in my throat.

"Of course, sure dad, that would be just peachy keen, nifty." What else could I say, this was a nice restaurant and I didn't want to make a scene and I was so enjoying my lunch. I could bail out on the topic at a later date, if it's ever brought up again. We finished up our food. Dad and Barry split the bill and headed back to drop me off at my place, our place?

Not five minutes after Barry and Dad dropped me off and pulled away from the curb, did Braiden magically appear. That was a close call. I was sitting on the front step.

"Hi honey" Braiden said rather loudly as he stepped out of the car.

"Hi back at cha"" I think I sounded festive enough. He got right up close to kiss me hello.

"What's this in your hair? It looks like a small tentacle?" he pulled it off me and examined it closer.

"Yes, it's a tentacle, I had lunch with my Dad and his work buddy Barry, I bet you're sorry you missed out on that?"

Braiden snapped back sarcastically. "Yeah, real sad I'm real bummed out." Convincing? I think not. "So, why'd he come over?" he continued to ask.

"I am not entirely sure? He either, missed me and wanted to hang out or Effie finally cracked and spilled the proverbial "shacking up" beans. I personally think Effie ratted me out and

I intend to confront her about it when she gets home from work before Patrick gets home. He'll just get in the way and defend her. He is such a gallant gentleman protecting his lady, he isn't aware of all the shit she has pulled in her life. Let him keep the illusion." I folded my arms as if to make my words more effective.

"Well I know she gets off early today I over heard her on the phone when I was hanging out with Patrick last night, so I am going up stairs, take a shower and a nap. When I get up let's go out to dinner, you pick. Try to be gentle, when you're grilling your sister. Okay?" he kissed me and headed up the stairs to wash the day away.

And what impeccable timing she has. At that moment strangely enough Effie drove up in her very new car? I wonder how she afforded the down payment. Although I think I already had my answer. My, I was having a lot of epiphanies today. "Hi Effie, nice car, shit, how'd you afford that? What did you have to sell this time, your soul? Or just rat out your little sister, you incompetent slut!" She was only slightly stunned as I imagined she was probably prepared for this moment.

"Look you little shit; it was for your own good. You're way too young to be trying to play house with a man. You're immature and self absorbed and you can't even hold down a real job. I mean really you only recently learned to do the laundry. You need to move back home and get your life together and out of my sight for a while. I can't be responsible for you and I am tired of covering your ass! Besides that I would now say we're even for screwing up each others love lives! As you'll recall I was set to elope with Steve a few years ago and you told Mom and Dad." Her voice was at a strict elevated tone, but the neighbors still couldn't quite hear us. Luckily I was polite enough to accommodate them and turn up the volume when I replied.

"Listen you naive tramp, Steve was a jerk, he was engaged to another woman and he was using you. Besides, what business is it of yours as to how I am running or ruining my own life? And after all you're a horrible excuse for a role model as a big sister.

You're the one who I smoked my first joint with. You even took me on dates with you for chaperoning. So don't you lecture me on how to be a model citizen, maybe I will listen to you once you can get your own shit together."

About then she started to cry, the neighbors peeked out of their doors and Braiden came running down the stairs wrapped in a bath towel. I had struck a nerve! I felt like wanting to beat my chest and make superior ape noises. I had won the battle and my adrenalin was in full force, as my breathing became heavy and I swear I let out a snorting sound? Braiden grabbed my arm and dragged me back up the stairs so I wouldn't cause any more of a scene. Dear sister had run into her apartment wailing and slammed the door behind her. Dramatically I might add. I was sure I would be getting a call soon from our loving parents. Ring ,ah yes Ring, went the unfriendly sound of the phone. Not wanting to answer it but I felt whoever it was would just not let up unless they spoke their peace.

"Hello? Oh, hi, Mom, and how are you on this lovely day, doing well I hope? "I held the receiver a good foot away from my ear as she started yelling into it.

"You hurt your sister's feelings…blah blah blah you little tramp!,…blah, blah blah,….incoherent babble and some more insults and then…he is no good, no good I tell you… I even had a chat with his overeducated mother!…some more insults and a little swearing, Good-by!"

Okay that was a blast. Love you to mom. She had already hung up but I felt a need to say it. Ring and ring again! I could tell that the phone would be bringing me tidings of great joy this afternoon. "Hello?" I was ever cautious, "Oh, hi there Mrs. Hostettler, No Bray cant make it to the phone right now he is in the shower can I pass on a message? … Oh you want him to call you as soon as possible. Yes I can pass on the message; you have a nice day too." Fuck! This was just a bit more than I cared to deal with at this moment but of course you guessed it, a knock on the door from Patrick the brave and true!

"Hello Pat, nice to see you. Would you like to come in for a beverage? Or perhaps some cake?" I sounded as falsely hospitable as possible. Motioning him into the living room where he proceeded to scold me like a child bringing home an "F" in phys ed. on his report card. Funny, I know exactly how that feels as I used to fail P.E. at every turn. I am not an athletic type. In fact I had to take two consecutive periods of phys-ed in my senior year or they would not let me graduate.

Anyway back to Patrick and I braced myself for the finger pointing session.

"How dare you speak to your sister that way, she has done nothing but support your sorry ass all her life. She is a saint! She would never do anything to hurt anyone, you, ungrateful little snot. What have you got to say for yourself? You have to go down and apologize to her right this minute missy!"

Excuse me did he just call me missy? "Listen "Pops" you have no idea what you're saying. I have spent more time with that woman than you have and you're just blinded by the free sex. So don't call her a saint because although she is many things, that the one thing she is not. I refuse to apologize. I have nothing to apologize for. I have done nothing wrong and she got a new car out of the deal. Of which I am sure Daddy footed the bill for that." So, there that ought to teach him.

"Hey wait a minute I am the one who gave her the down payment for the car. Hers' was costing way too much in repairs and was not a sound investment. She needed a good car to get her to and from work and I just got a raise. So you really do need to say you're sorry if that's the impression you got."

Okay so I could be wrong about that one. "Hey, I am still not going to speak to her, she did tell on me and I refuse to have anything more to do with her or you for that matter." I stood firm on this and of course Braiden came stomping out into the living room. This time at least he had his pants on.

"Hey Pat quit yelling at Doris, it's not her fault and I would appreciate it if you would just go back down stairs until all of us can discuss this like rational humans." Braiden had him by the shoulder and scooted him out the door.

"My hero!" I said as he shut the door.

"Hero,...yah, right. Look you know your going to have to go say you're sorry, don't you? Avoiding an unpleasant conversation is never the right thing to do."

I was staring down at my feet but answered sheepishly "Yes, you're right I will. But I am going to let her stew a little while before I do, because after all she did sing like a canary to Mom and Dad. But I suppose in a way I deserved it." I admit when I am wrong, it's difficult and it's not often, but I do.

"Oh, Bray speaking of unpleasant avoidance your mother called and she wants you to call her right away." He looked at me as if to say you must be joking.

"I'll call her later when I feel like talking to her or maybe I won't call her at..." I glared at him and he picked up the phone and dialed. "Hi Dad? Could you put Mom on the phone, she asked me to call.

"Hi mom, yes I know. Yes I am aware of the situation. No, I am sorry to hear that. I am sure it was an unpleasant interaction for you and Doris' mother. Yes, you knew that...I told you weeks ago, yes I did. Look I know this will all blow over and you won't get anymore calls from her...me too, bye." Bray hung up, let out a large sigh and went back to the bedroom to finish getting dressed.

I sat on the couch with arms folded trying to figure out what my next move would be. I could run away, but no one would notice? Sure they would notice, because I am there main source of entertainment and they'd miss me. Where else could they misplace their anger, and blatant hostility? Just because they had crappy boring responsible lives, is it any reason to take it out on me? Fresh out of ideas, my brain was bored now with the whole ordeal and I was in desperate need of a joint. I headed to the bedroom where I found Braiden who still no shirt on just laying on the bed staring blankly at the ceiling.

"We have any weed left?" I asked moving around the pillow on the chair in the corner and then looking into the shoebox he kept under the bed.

"No, we're out. I have been thinking maybe we should stop smoking the stuff." He was still staring at the ceiling. What was up with him? What was this nonsense talk all about?

"Give it up? At this moment in my life it was the only thing keeping me from jumping off the roof. Are you feeling okay? Oh I remember I always keep an emergency doobie in my jewelry case. Yes there it is!" I lit up and looked over at Braiden and something was defiantly bugging him. "So, tell me what's going on." I scooted the chair over to the bed where I could prop up my feet on it and stare at him.

" I don't know what I am doing anymore, I have lost direction. I need a change of surroundings. There is really nothing here for us now. And your parents are freaking out. Maybe everyone is right and I am a bad influence on you? I am having that crisis in life when a man wants to make something more for himself." I handed him the reefer, and as took a hit off of it he sat up on the bed and blurted out. "I want to go to Alaska I want you with me and it seems like the only choice we have if we are going to stay together."

Ah, I knew this was coming I could feel it. "Listen I care about you a lot, you know that. I just don't think I am wilderness material. I'm sure not Annie Oakley.

I 'm not even like that Engalls-Wilder chick on "Little House on the Prairie". Maybe you need to go without me." I was starting to get a wee bit light and airy now. Braiden sitting on the bed without his shirt on was not helping me focus on the topic at hand. With those long thin muscular arms, those deep brown eyes and hey I could go for a roll in the hay right about now. So I parked the joint on the ashtray and lunged for him.

"Really, I am serious, are you listening to me. Stop that, it tickles, I mean it. Oh, yeah that feels pretty good." Needless to say his protest was short lived and well one thing led to another.

He did keep talking and kissing at the same time. Those hot sweet lips and warm breath were a good combination.

"We could go up north to just check it out. We don't have to have a time schedule to keep, we can just go see what its like. Oh like that oh, keep doing that, wow."

I was kind of pre occupied at the moment and decided to just say " Yes, what ever you want, yes, that would be good, very good." By this time I had really forgot what we were talking about in the first place and I am sure Braiden would refresh my memory at a later time. So I stayed involved in the activity at hand. The moment our interlude had ended I regained my brain cells and turned to him lying there.

"Alaska? Did I say I would go with you to Alaska? I must be insane. Can we go out for some ice cream now?" I had to laugh as I am screwed for agreeing to this. "Yes, I guess we are going and I guess we can go get some ice cream."

CHAPTER NINE
"Tripping North"

In what I must call a rather feeble attempt to alleviate the mounting tension between Effie, Patrick, and everyone concerned I reluctantly moved back into my parents' house. This seemed to appease Braiden's' mother and father, and my own as well. This was a delaying tactic until Bray and I could carry out our planned escape.

Running away seems like the best idea we could come up with. I had not informed my mother yet. She was still reeling from the whole cats out of the bag issue. I was a tainted woman now so she had to come to grips with that. If I dropped the reality bomb that I was leaving it would prove too much for her, I am certain. Finding out I was a wanton woman was bound to happen. Braiden and I tried to hide it for too long and I am surprised it took this long to hit the fan.

No matter, my mother was very upset. Now the parents seemed to band together to break us apart thinking it was all in our best interest. I was too young and easy to manipulate and he was too sophisticated and worldly for me.You know how that one goes. So I moved back home until things had cooled down enough to break the news of my impending departure. Since being ratted out by my dear sister, I really had nothing left to loose. I am kind of relieved that much was out in the open. Now all I had to do was find a graceful way to say. "Hey, I am getting my ass out of Dodge and heading to the final frontier!" Or is that the last frontier? I guess it's all the same thing cold and unknown territory.

When I broke the news to my father of my plans to go to Alaska with Braiden he did not seem the least bit as shocked as I thought he would. He looked at me as if he thought I was bluffing. I always had hated camping and outdoors, my black hair was always neatly styled or permed, nails always polished and my outfits properly co-coordinated. I who practically invented sports shopping, wrestling for the last hand bag on sale and snapping up a pair of red satin shoes even if I would never have any occasion to wear them, just so as no one else could own them.

Because of that selfish streak in me, perfecting the art of mall Olympics was where I showed my talent. Since my ancestors invented the Olympics who better to elevate mall Olympics to a whole new level than.

I tried fishing with my father a couple of times.In my family everyone was encouraged to either learn hunting or fishing. I chose fishing because it seemed less brutal. On one occasion dad and I went to fish off the dock in Martinez. We sat there about an hour until I started screaming and flailing and jumping up and down as my dad ran over pulled my pole out from the water and there was no fish. He was puzzled and I was crying while explaining.

"No, not a fish, I was stung by something, ouch, ouch. " sob, and sniffle, I was stung by a yellow jacket, actually I some how sat on a yellow jacket. I was in pain, so dad put me in the car got our fishing gear and drove us home. We never tried fishing together again after that.

Dad agreed living in the wild would prove to be a good learning experience for me, whether I made it back home alive or not was beside the point. I had taken him out to our favorite burger place to get a bite and talk things out with him. I had hardly been home a week before I broke the news.

"Doris I am not the least bit shocked" he said in his monotone voice, "There is nothing you have ever done or ever will do that will surprise me. You have always been a shit disturber and I mean that in the most endearing way possible. I know you see something in this Braiden person and as difficult as it is for me to accept that I cannot fight you. This trip is going to be shock to your system and I also think you may find out a few things about yourself. I am not pleased you're going, but it's your decision. I will stand behind it. And I hope that there will not be much fishing involved." He was being supportive and just a little bit tongue in cheek with that last remark. I got it and we had a nice little chuckle. We agreed to be friends and I agreed to call him if I got in a bind up there. We also agreed it would probably be best not to tell mom. The actual plan was to tell her right as I was getting in the car to leave so she would have little time to vocalize her opinion.

So, when do you leave?" Dad asked. "A week from today, Lars got us a special airfare, so we take something called "the red-eye" to arrive in Seattle at midnight. Then we hop on the ferry in the early morning, around 9am? I think? Then we head to Ketchikan." I said trying to sound like the big shot that I wasn't.

Get a load of me, the seasoned world traveler. I was heading into what was perceived as no mans land. The final frontier, no it was the last frontier. Space is the final frontier. Thank Star Trek for that one. Who was I kidding? I had not ever been really far from home before. The longest trip away was to camp Loma Mar when I was a youngster. I wasn't totally sure I could successfully wipe my own ass at this point.

Finally the day arrived. I had not slept more than an hour total, at intervals of ten minutes at a time. My mind raced and heart pounded as I thought what am I doing? How am I going to manage this? Or worse, how can I get to the car and out of here without Mom catching me?

This will be as much fun as a tooth extraction without having your nerves deadened first. I have not experienced this but I read somewhere that in the Old West days, the dentist would just put his knee on your chest and rip out the tooth with a hand held metal device while you were conscious. I have to believe that some times the patient would be drunker than a teenager with a fake ID in a nightclub with dollar drinks

. The morning was beautiful, seven thirty am. It was warm, sunny and unseasonably perfect. It was great weather to travel in. I had coffee and a piece of toast as my mother stared coldly at me. I should have known Dad could not keep quiet. Her gaze was unsettling. Maybe I should not have even told Dad. It was a little late for me to take that one back. Oh well. I packed up the last of my things and headed for the door to pack my car.

I loaded up my economical and safe 1978 AMC Hornet Sportabout, a really spiffy car I may add. All my friends owned muscle cars and sports cars and one even owned a Lincoln Continental with suicide doors. That was a most righteous ride. My car was probably the reason I dated guys with great cars. Hey, it ran.

Here it is nine am on a breathtaking Saturday morning in our quiet, very quiet upper middle class suburban neighborhood. You could literally hear a pin drop if in fact someone was using it and dropped it. My father followed me out to see if I needed help and to slip me 200 bucks cash and a check for another $500 to open an account when I got up there.

"Gee, thanks Dad" I said gleefully but that glee was to be short lived as here comes mother. Hell hath no fury like a pissed off mom.

"Just when did you plan on informing me? You rotten good for nothing little tramp." My mother was yelling at the top of her lungs. "Were you just going to run off with that jackass and not say anything? Had you even planned to write? I'm cutting you out of the will. Do you hear me?"

"Gee mom, the whole fucking neighborhood can hear you,

probably all of Walnut Creek can hear you!" I screamed back. Lights started to come on in neighboring homes. "That's it I smart mouthed my mother I am officially going to hell". My Father looked quite mortified and told me to just get in the car and go. That he would calm down Mom.

"Jesus, Helen get back in the house you're making a scene" (Oh that's good Dad, way to calm Mom down).

Needless to say I sped out of there like the proverbial bat outta hell you hear so much about. I had never seen my mother this angry. Sure the past few holidays she has raised a fuss. It does seem odd that only in the time that I had started my relationship with Braiden has she really wanted to call attention to herself. That's it she's gone mad. Or it could be that change of life thing?

I arrived at Braiden's parents house, he moved back in with them as well. It was more cost effective, he saved up some more money for our adventure and also he let the apartment go because Effie and Patrick were now officially an item out in the open. Mom and Dad were at lot easier on their co-habitat-ional arrangement.

We took a taxi from Braiden's ' house to the airport. I left my car for Patrick and Effie to use while we were away. Since all the shit hit the fan and cleared the air, Effie and I were on speaking terms once again, limited but effective. This was in effects ever since she heard I was leaving, and that was a load off my mind. She also was going to aid Dad in keeping our Mother from blowing a gasket.

Braiden indicated we should eat something before we got on the plane. It was going to be a busy night. I wasn't that hungry but the plane ride to Seattle was short so there would be no food. Better safe than sorry. I am unsure how airport food really figures in to that saying? Better safe than sorry. It could mean that I eat now thinking I am safe and then I become sorry later? Anyway, airport food is much like the food you get at the snack bar of the drive in. Same quality just costs more. I chose a hot dog and a non caffeinated beverage.

As I ate my rubbery hot dog it finally dawned on me I was heading out on an adventure. An adventure as Ralph had predicted by Tarot cards so many months before. Would it be good? Bad? Life changing? Am I going to die up there? Am I going to have a tooth pulled out by a crazed dentist from the dark ages? I started to panic a little. I gasped in air and a bit of the hot dog lodged in my throat and I drank a swig of my watery soda to push it down before I turned a nice shade of blue. I eventually regained some of my composure and just then Braiden pulls this little baggy out of his pocket to discreetly show me.

"Hey, I brought some coke." He said in a hushed voice as he glanced around nonchalantly. I must admit cocaine freaks me out a little bit. Pot is easy going, cheap and will just make you mellow. No big deal. Cocaine on the other hand is expensive, high profile and makes you very awake, nervous and hyper. Kind of like a Chihuahua caught in a blender, which is sick visual I have to admit. You get the general idea, as I do not mean literally in a blender. Being very hyper by nature (hyper ness runs in my family of all things to pass down.) it had to be neurosis and hyperactivity. It could not be math and science skills. Adding to the fact we as a whole are generally small in stature, it has just made matters worse. People tend to shun away from short nervous neurotic hyper people. Whoopee I hit the jackpot!

Braiden could snort it all if he wanted to, I however would stick to the weed. It was calmer and safer and in fact I am going to go to the ladies room now and puff a little before we boarded. The ladies room was empty and I managed a few hits before the overhead speaker announced it was time to head for Seattle.

Our plane was on time. We flew, I was in a plane! I was up in the air. I was excited. I had never been in a plane before. If you give it some thought planes are truly unnatural and it can bring on a rather helpless feeling if you're a worrier but can make you feel free if you're a thrill seeker. I am undecided as to which category I fall into. Braiden on the other hand slept the whole time that we were suspended in the air. Suspended like a tacky flying object you would notice in old science fiction movies hanging from threads as they move around a cardboard sky. Then we landed, oh joy of joys. Landing is something I believe everyone needs to experience. Taking off makes your body feel light, and the ascension into the clouds gives you a feeling of heading for heaven. Landing is the opposite of this and oddly enough, if it is a rough landing, it can make you feel as though you're going to be closer to heaven than take off.Anything that weighs as much as an aircraft meeting earth at an over accelerated speed with the added movement of bouncing can give you the impression you're nearer to the afterlife.

Braiden awoke refreshed and dare I say chipper. I however was not. By the time we arrived at the ferry terminal it was 6am, and I had been awake just over twenty-four hours straight. Not a big deal, I would sleep on the ferry. Then we got on the ferry and the operator said it would be about thirty-six hour ride to Ketchikan. The ferry was spectacular. Windows everywhere, no beds though. You could have a room for an extra $100, but Braiden did not feel we needed one. It would be more fun sleeping in the great room. It was the large part of the ferry where the bar was. It was crowded and the floor was hard. I felt like a refuge from some foreign country. My enthusiasm was waning. I did not sleep. I laid there all night long looking out the window at the multitude of starts passing over head.

Morning came around much too fast. We went into the dining area and I ate a little but was more excited and exhausted than hungry. I was heading into the 48 hour mark of being awake and not just awake I was freaky adrenalin hyped up awake. By now Braiden noticed I didn't look so well. There was no place to lie down so we kept busy all day watching the killer whales and sea lions swim by. I walked in a daze. Ah, finally nighttime, sleep time! Or was it? I wasn't sure any longer. I was starting to lose it and royally. I had lain down for a while, but the sleep fairy did not visit. Instead I was being bypassed so he could bestow his gift of easy rest and replenishment onto people around me. I instead became the unwilling designated night watchman keeping the flocks from being devoured by intruders. Sleep well weary travelers; fret not as I will tend guard.

I decided all by myself to go up on deck and partake of the cool night air. Yes, a walk is just what I needed. I got up slipping out of the sleeping bag ever so gently so as not to wake Braiden. No one moved, I heard a few snores and irregular breathing from the other passengers on the floor, but no one was the slightest bit startled or showed any need to awaken from the cocoons they were in. The power of the ferry along with its rocking in the water seemed to be enough to keep them in a semi-comatose state. The night air was pleasant, albeit chilly enough to make a polar bear ask for a sweat suit for Christmas. But I can handle it. I was alone on deck, alone in my thoughts, and perhaps alone in the world or the universe at this moment, was this maybe a dream? If I was in a dream then if I throw myself overboard I would not die. I would wake up and see I had been asleep all this time. I swear I could hear the call of the sirens far off in the distance, like the sailors in mythological times. They were beckoning me. I would be safe with them they promised me, I heard them I did, and clearly. The moon overhead shined dimly on the dark water below and looked inviting to a tormented soul. Even with the limited lighting I found it fairly easy to make out the shapes of the black and white mermaids swimming past me. I will join them I will become one with the ocean. I will become a sad story that people will pass down from generation to generation. I will be immortal. Braiden being sound asleep also maybe he was in bed next to me and as I hit the water I will wake up in our bed together and I will laugh. "Ha!" The laugh was audible which must have meant I was out of my mind. I threw my leg up to the railing and at mid-point sat there teetering and holding on precariously as Braiden came bolting onto the deck to grab me and pull me back.

"Hey, I was going to be immortal why did you stop me and why do you feel so real if I am dreaming? If I didn't know better I'd say were both awake."

Braiden held me for a few moments "What the hell are you doing here? Why were you on the railing? Why are you out here in the cold?" sensing a disturbance one of the deckhands came out to offer assistance.

"Excuse me my name is Steve, are you two okay? Is there a problem? Can I be of any assistance?"

Braiden continued to hold onto me and replied for the both of us as I stared at the multitude of stars. "Hi Steve, there is no problem. We were just getting some air and taking a little walk. You know how cold air feels good on an upset stomach,." Braiden sort of insinuated we were seasick. That was less shocking and disturbing than the truth of "Hey, well my girlfriend was wigging out and I came to pull her off the rail so she wouldn't throw herself overboard into the depths of the abyss." We stayed on deck for a few more minutes until the bone numbing cold made its presence known. "Are you better now? Shall we go back inside and try to sleep again?" I nodded, too cold to open my mouth. I had to keep my teeth clenched or else they would chatter and break off. Braiden escorted me back to our warm cozy makeshift bed and hung on to me all the while.

Braiden looked scared and helpless all at once, not knowing what to do with me. I was starting to panic again, and this time I was developed a glazed look. "Bray, honey." I said in a hushed voice "Their ridiculing us, I hear them, don't you hear them talking about us? They are making plans." I said like a person who talks to cabbage.

"Who is honey?" Braiden said reassuringly. I proceeded with "Bray, I cant sleep, I will never sleep again, there going to take you away, the Coast Guard is coming and their going to take you away because you have drugs on you, they know it, they have been watching us. You have to get rid of it. If you don't they'll come get you, they will take you away and I will never see you again." I truly was convinced, and apparently I was convincing. Because at that point my dear shaken up pillar of strength got up and left the communal sleeping quarters for what seemed like twenty or so minutes. I laid there in all my paranoid wonder and waited for his return.

"Its okay its gone the stuff is gone I threw it over board. Now just lay here with me if you can't sleep, I'll take care of you until the morning. We're fine, we'll be okay now, everything is fine. " With his arms wound tightly around me, I closed my eyes but did not sleep. Instead my disassociated crazed mind entertained itself with gentle delusions and comforting insanity, while others around me enjoyed their peaceful slumber. Oh, how I would envy them, if I was in my right mind.

Morning arrived once again. Bray and I ate a light breakfast of juice and pastries. I had to forgo the coffee, caffeine and all. Then he parked me by a wall out of the way of any traffic where he felt I'd be safe. And not bring harm to the sane passengers while he went to talk to the crewman on deck. I noticed some passer's by would point and whisper to their companions and I got the feeling our friend Steve had a whale of a tale to spread. The wear and tear on Braiden was taking its toll and he had finally had enough of all this. His idea was to arrange for me to sleep in one of the deckhand rooms. His brother was friends with some of the ferry workers and even if he had to slip them a few bucks it was well worth it. In the meantime I leaned against the cold wall.

Eventually being approached by a really well dressed and neatly shaven man who looked me straight in the eyes and said "My dear I have watched you since we boarded, and you look very troubled. I would like to help you. Here is my card I am staying in stateroom #307,if you need anything at all." He was very sweet and handsome and his card said he was a psychiatrist. Was it that obvious? Of course it was. He patted me on the shoulder and walked off as Braiden came around the corner to witness this.

"Who was that very friendly looking older man? Was he a pervert? Should I contact someone? I leave you alone for five minutes and …oh?" Braiden stopped as I handed him the card. He read it and remarked. "Imagine that?" Then he sort of chuckled "God works in mysterious ways. Now come with me, we are going to the bar. Where I am going to pour liquor down your throat until you pass out, that's the plan."

All the words I was able to put together were "Sounds like a good one." I drank several Tom Collins because they are my favorite drink, and then I was directed to the loaned stateroom, where I, with great relief passed out into a deep and long sleep. For those few hours, all was right with the world once again.

Aside from wasting $300 worth of cocaine and having a hallucinogenic episode it was a nice ride. And shortly we would be docking at Ketchikan. By the way, it's not a well known fact but Ketchikan is the salmon capitol of the modern world.

CHAPTER TEN

"It's too late to turn back now."

Yes! Land ho! At last we were docking. We had arrived and meet Braiden's older brother whose real name is Sigmund, like the sea monster on television. He prefers to be called "Zig" for obvious reasons. His girlfriend Terri, and Braiden's sister Valda had joined him greet us at the dock.

Luckily I had a chance to freshen up and change my clothing on the ferry, or I would have induced fright. I would have liked to fix my hair also because all the curl came out of it, but hey there wasn't enough time.

Braiden's brother Zig took us on a mini tour around the city, or was it a town? No, it's a city. Although not the definition I would use, because it's nowhere near the sprawling smog filled and litter laden ones that I am used to. We were informed that we would be staying with Zig's girlfriend Terri. Zig owned a float house but it would be too small for us all to stay in and I am guessing Zig preferred to stay on his own.

Ketchikan is an amazing place; there are 300 bars for a population of about 3,000 people. Okay, maybe I am exaggerating. The population was higher or lower depending on the time of year, still I may be wrong. The entire city spans approximately four or five miles. Most of the homes have such a rustic look and feel that you expected old gold miners to come walking out of them. The buildings that line most of the waterfront are up on stilts and can best be described as quaint and unreal. The whole business district consisted of two grocery stores, a newly built library, a movie theatre and rumor has it they were just about to start construction an a bowling alley. Whoopee! I must say I was more under-whelmed than impressed coming from an area that possessed all of this and more.

Braiden's' brother Zig was another story altogether. He was a looker, oh boy, with long blond curly hair like Roger Daltrey in "Tommy" but more rugged and outdoorsy. He spoke with a raspy gravely voice and his brown eyes seemed to dance and smile when he talked. I was impressed with this much older man of 27.

Terri was a very down to earth woman; in fact I would come to find out that most of the women in Ketchikan were, shall we say, unassuming. I was the exception to this and was determined to stay that way. They don't see the likes of my kind here much, unless they were coming off a cruise ship. Compared to these women I seemed prissy and weak. Terri was pleasant and kind and sweet by nature, but had an air of toughness about her. And as petite as Terri was you knew she could hold her own against anybody, man or woman or elk for that matter. With her shoulder length brown hair, no make up, wearing jeans, boots and a man's flannel shirt over a white t-shirt, I had no idea then that I would come to idolize and fashion myself after her.

Dear sister Val looked just like a blend between Zig and Braiden, on the thin side, with long golden blonde hair and vivid green eyes.Even without any makeup on she looked like a model, just stunning. One of those natural beauties you hear so much about but rarely ever encounter. When she laughed I would imagine she would warm up an entire room, or in this case the small station wagon we were all riding in

. "How much further is our destination? I am a sort of hungry." I tried to be relaxed about asking, but I really wanted out of this car. I had been traveling for so long and I just wanted to not be moving any longer. If I had been a pioneer in the old west time riding in a covered wagon I would have shot the driver by now and eaten a prairie dog. But our driver was much too cute and I was sure someone would take pity on us and feed us soon.

I was informed that the men outnumbered the women by a large margin of at least five to one. It was hard not to notice that everywhere I looked there were men. Some tall, some not so tall, there were older men and younger men and it was like a smorgasbord of the testosterone variety. Most of them good looking and built like the mountains they came from. Val and Terri informed me quietly that dating around here was like a feeding frenzy at a piranha tank. We were having a giggle in the back seat at this and at that time the car stopped. It stopped at what looked like a building promising of food! Yes, hooray we were going to eat.

"Let's feed you two and then head on home. The food on the ferry is never very good although decent. But this place will make you comfortable and the food is really hearty and homemade. I was expecting the menu to have; oh I don't know moose or bear on it and maybe some tree bark as a side dish. Luckily I was wrong and I had a juicy steak made from a real cow with a baked potato and leafy green salad. And a root beer! I was in heaven. This restaurant didn't look impressive by any standards, it was understated and surprised you with its charm. Much like I was starting to find that the people up here did as well.

When we finally did make it up to Terri's' place I was exhausted but I did my best to stay up and converse a little. After all it was the social thing to do. Terri's place was inviting, with blankets thrown over the chair and back of the big over stuffed couch, for those nights when you wished to cozy up. The living room had two very large windows that overlooked the downtown and partial view of the waterway. The kitchen although not up to date, was neat and clean and had a country look to it with pictures of rooster's and a few old plates on the walls. The only bathroom in the apartment consisted of a pedestal sink and a claw footed tub. And thank the lord an indoor toilet. I was expecting some wood structure out back with a moon carved into the door. The whole place was cute and surprisingly I felt relaxed in what I would call home for the duration of our stay. Yes, the accommodations would do just fine thank you very much.

Terri and I and Val sat down at the kitchen table while Zig and Braiden sat on the bar stools next to us at the counter. "When you two get settled in and sometime over the next few days we'd like to take you over to the float house near Pennock. Also there are a lot of parties coming up where you can meet some people and get used to your new surroundings if that sounds good to you both?" Zig asked politely and the girls were in agreement.

Braiden said "Sure that sounds great. Of course I want to look for a job right away. I would love to get out on a fishing excursion with you Zig if you would help me?"

Zig smiled and patted Braiden on the shoulder. "Yeah I can manage that little brother. You want a beer? Anyone else want a beer?" there was a collective "Yes, me please" I even partook of one. "So, you two don't need to worry about rent, but I would appreciate it if you could help clean up once in a while and do some chores, and if you want to pitch in for food. It will keep us all friends here."

Terri smiled and took a swig of beer. "That seems more than fair and we really are grateful for all your kindness. Aren't we Doris?"

I felt this was quite fair. "Yes, of course it seems more than fair. Now if you will excuse me I think it's defiantly time for bed. Where do we sleep?"

Terri pointed to the door off the kitchen it was her second bedroom. "Make yourself at home and we will try and keep it down out here. Good night Doris, see you in the morning."

Then Val and Zig added "Were glad you're here, see you in the morning." Braiden and Val and Zig and Terri all stayed up to talk. I was looking so forward to a real bed and a real night's sleep. This was going to be good I can tell, the bed was a queen size with a white and brass accent headboard and a fluffy comforter on top. With lots of pillows and also in the room was a big rocking chair and antique dresser. I would have plenty of time to converse and interact in the days to come. Now was not the time. It was the time to introduce myself to my new best friends, a pillow and blanket that awaited me.

Braiden didn't get on a fishing boat as they were already staffed with crew, he was told if someone got sick or backed out or died then he could get on the list. He instead got a job at the local taxi cab company The Samuel-Titan. It's a weird cab company, there are only three cabs and all of them painted an ugly orange color and resemble giant crabs so I took to calling it the "Crab Cab." One of taxis' had a twisted fender with a tennis shoe stuck in it. I never did figure out what was up with that name either. It sounded more like a beer company. Which reminded me that a beer sounded good along with a nice loaf of bread and crab dip? But that could just be my stomach talking.

I was curious as to what Braiden did all day. Well aware that it involved charging fifty dollars for driving tourists around the city all day. But what did one get for that fifty dollar tour? I wanted to know. So he agreed to take me out during his lunch break. We stopped and picked up a couple of sandwiches and drinks and off we went to a place known as Totem Bight. It was one of the more interesting spots in this God forsaken territory. Real totem poles and get this, Indians actually made them. Not some Hollywood movie set. These are works of art and impressive. One of them I swear was at least 50 feet high, or maybe it just dwarfed me. I used to think that no such things could exist. That someone made up the story of these monoliths. Carved wooden statues? Come on? Not possible. But no, they were real and I was touching them. No one would ever believe I had seen this. It was bizarre to say the least, but in a fascinating way.

Usually they were overrun by snapshot tourists. It was quiet and peaceful this time. No, at this moment it was just Braiden and I and the Totems and lunch. I was feeling some odd new sensation and could not readily identify it, but I believe its called inner peace. No smelly auto exhaust fumes, no sirens or loud noises, it was nice as we sat there in silence just eating and smiling at each other and the beautiful bird chirping infused trees. I was in touch with my deeper being and I was actually kind of digging it, I could have stayed in this spot in time forever. Unfortunately our lunch interlude was coming to a close and Braiden had to get the cab back into action.

As we sat in the front seat almost ready to leave. Braiden put his left hand to my face and kissed me in the sweetest most romantic way he had ever done. Romance was generally not part of our interactions. They were usually more primal and to the point. No flirting, no gentle touches. This was a refreshing new twist, but I got the feeling somehow it would be a short lived addition because our time up here was more controlled and orchestrated, both by others demands on us and the demands we had to impose on ourselves.

"What was that for?" I asked with a simple smile creeping over my face.

"Nothing in particular, I am just glad to be up here and grateful you're here with me." I was touched at his saying this. Could he actually be ready to tell me sometime soon that he, do I dare think it, loves me? The ride back to town was pleasant and the trees lining the road were greener shade than I had ever seen before. Well I must admit I never really encountered a lot of trees back home. Well, except for the few that line the streets, or if you make a special trip through the great redwoods. Come to think of it the air up here smelled better and also the stress levels were of a different kind. Worry up here was for different reasons, not so selfish and single minded. You had a job for simple basic reasons to buy groceries or pay rent and that was about it. No one was trying to out do one another and the idea of competitive spirit gave way to support for the other persons endeavors and dreams.

We made it back to the center of town where Braiden had to drop me off. He kissed me once more. "Thanks for the nice romantic lunch." I smirked and he grinned back. "I should be home early today I get off at about four. Terri won't be home until later or tomorrow morning she is staying with Zig. You know what that means?"

Yes, as a matter of fact I did, you sly dog. And it would be the first time in the three and a half weeks since we got up here. The longest we had ever been without sex. "Yeah, I am looking forward to it; bring home some pizza so we don't have to go out at all." I winked as he drove away.

I thought it's a good time for a walk to get the mail before I head back to the apartment, to get ready for a steamy night. I like to take my walk to the post office box every other day to break the monotony. Because Braiden was working most all day every day, I had been filling my time by looking for decent employment when I wasn't going to the P.O. Box or goofing off with the friends we had made. I felt a walk was in order and the rest of the afternoon was my own, for the most part. I had applied everywhere that was hiring. I had cleaned the apartment this morning before I left and Braiden would be around to play after four o'clock. So I was on my own. This day was breathtaking, clouds dotted the sky and a cool breeze came off the water. The walk down through the town was a winding one I had to pass a lot of the shops and businesses on the way and waved at most of the owners because it's a small place and I am getting to know everyone.

I walked into Terri's' coffee shop to see how she was doing. Once in a while Terri would let me run the place so she could take a break. I know she did it to make me feel useful like I was contributing. She had her own apartment, her own store and she was self sufficient. It was clear she loved Zig, it was also clear she didn't need any man. The coffee shop is cozy, about the size of a phone booth, an American one not a British one. I just feel the USA has to have the biggest of everything. There are three tables and a few chairs and she stocks little incidental items like toothpaste and shampoo. It's like Ketchikan's answer to a convenience store without the frozen drink machine.

"Hey there, you left before I got up this morning I missed our coffee klatch!" Terri was reading the newspaper as I entered. "Are you on the way to the post office?

I said "You know it and then the "Spaghetti Tree" for a pineapple shake. I cleaned the apartment and folded the laundry. I just had lunch with Braiden and he is coming home early at four today. What time are you going over to Zig's tonight?" I wanted to know so we could all maybe have a drink together before we all did our separate things.

"I'll be home at three thirty to get some overnight things. How about you and I go to the Rusty Pelican, so we I could have a drink together and chat before we have to meet the guys?"

I nodded in reply and said it sounded like a plan. "I've got this extra mint sail, you want it?" she asked knowing full well what the answer was. I loved these things they were like a brownie but with a mint frosting. Extra one, sure yeah I know she was just saving it for me and of course with a cup of coffee it was the perfect snack. This wonderful women was my friend and I was proud of that. With a mouth full of mint sail I mumbled "Buyff" and went on my merry little way.

I would have to call Braiden and convey the slight change of plans but it would not interfere too much with our mating dance. He would be fine with meeting at the "Pelican" for a drink with Zig and Terri. I continued on my way strolling along at a relaxed pace and eventually I would arrive at the post office. I had never had a P.O. Box before and it was something that made me feel important in a way. You can imagine rock stars and celebrities and successful people having them to keep the common folks away, never knowing exactly where you lived would make it all the more difficult to stalk you.

I developed a game to opening the box, as I turn the key I try to speculate weather there will be any mail, and who it could be from. Like a coin toss only heads or tails becomes full or empty and the prize if mail exists. I am loved and if it's empty I am not. Just a sick mind trip I like to play with myself.

Dad would write to me often. We had been up here less than a month and already he had written three times. I still had not found a job, I kept trying. Dad enclosed a check for one hundred dollars this time. As I sat waiting for my spaghetti and pineapple shake. I read my letter.

Dear Nannook! Hope this letter finds you well and not frozen in a snow drift somewhere? The weather here is sunny eighty-five degrees and dry. Same as it always is, really quite boring. Your mother shows her love and support for you by not writing and by walking around the house cursing. Would you like me to send you anything? I know you're in an uncivilized area of the world and I can send you provisions and some meat products I can strap them to a Saint Bernard and have him deliver them. Effie and Patrick are getting married I thought you should know, but I'm not sure if your invited? Your sister will finally have a married name. I think Effie O'Malley has an odd ring to it. Poor thing, after all the hard work she has put in trying to land a man, she finally succeeded.

The ceremony will be in October and your mother is not thrilled about it because it means she has to find a dress. Effie won't have to find a dress though I think she purchased one when she was sixteen in anticipation. Okay I know that wasn't nice. Well I have enclosed a check for $10. ! Only kidding it's for a hundred and don't make a mistake and cash it for ten! Until our paths cross again, or you write asking for something. Bye for now.

Love "Papa"

P.S. say the word and I'll send you a plane ticket home.

Aw dad, that was nice. But I had every intention of sticking this out, seeing it through. On the way back after purchasing my pineapple shake and a newspaper as well as getting a message to Braiden about meeting Terri and I for drinks, I decided to sit on the bench at the dock. As I gazed out over the waterway that seemed still today I pondered my life once again and thought of Effie and Patrick's impending nuptials.Good for them. They deserve each other, and I mean that in the most heartfelt way. I sipped my shake and read all of the newspaper.

It came time to head back to the apartment to get dressed and ready to for drinks. Terri had arrived to grab a toothbrush and nightgown. Terri and I hung out and waited for the guys. The Rusty Pelican was very casual but the reason we liked it was the back deck that looked out over the water and had that feeling that you were at your friend's house just hanging out. Not at all pretentious, but it was very lively. Terri bought me as beer.

No one bothered two women sitting having drinks, the men were respectful and having them approach us without any invitation was a rare occurrence. So I was not in danger of any tempting hanky panky or of being busted on a technicality. But the men were enticing. I also had become friends with most of them so it was no biggy. I was assimilating into my new environment.

"I must say you look marvelous this evening, Terri. Trying to impress Zig?" I wanted to flatter her. She did look nice and who knows if either of the guys would say anything.

"Why thank you kindly my dear, you look nice as well. Zig is heading out for a five day fishing trip tomorrow and I am hoping he'll want me to stay over before he leaves in the morning." I figured it was something like that.

"Yeah, I figured it was something like that. Braiden and I have some plans of our own." So there we sat, two women with ulterior motives on our mind. We waited and drank until our unsuspecting prey arrived, like a couple of praying mantis.

Braiden and Zig sat down next to us each with beer in hand

and we all made polite conversation, letting the anticipation of a sexual encounter stew in the backs of all our minds.

"Zig, what's it really like on a fishing boat? Is it dangerous? Do you get tired of all the male companionship after a few hours?" I asked and sipped my bottle.

"It's pretty grueling, backbreaking work; I would not recommend it for everyone. And yea, you kind of get tired of each other being in such confined quarters day after day with just smelly sweaty men."

I was becoming intrigued and slightly aroused at the thought of a bunch of sweaty he-men, muscles rippling from throwing the nets out, the fishing lines becoming tight and having to use brut force to pull them in and the release of all those fish onto the deck. Oh, yea I am ready now.

"Wow, yawn I am really tired for some reason. Bray I think it's time to call it a night and head for bed." I grabbed his leg under the table and squeezed his thigh.

He understood immediately and needed no further prompting. "Hey, what do you know I am tired as well, hate to break up the party but you understand right Zig?"

To which the reply from Zig was. "Right Bray, I think Terri and I are quite tired as well. Hurry up and finish your beer Terri, and let's go."

CHAPTER ELEVEN

"Call of the Library"

I was working at Terri's coffee shop more often now. I had given up on looking for employment and Braiden was not pleased with this but said nothing. He was probably too tired from working to mention it, or pick an argument with me. We had not had sex since the evening we had drinks at the "Pelican" and it was less than satisfying. It was less than magical and he seemed distant, or preoccupied. Something had defiantly changed between us I just wasn't sure what caused it. Maybe it was overwork or stress, or possibly he was bored with me? The next morning and ever since then, he had just worked the night shift leaving at ten pm and getting in at eight am the next morning.

I was told by Terri that on occasion he would take the locals out to Totem Bight on a tour? Why? Was I missing something? When he was around he was no fun to be around. In fact I spent a lot of time alone. Sure I had made lots of friends but they had jobs and things to do. I did hang out with them a lot in the evenings and an occasional lunch, but for the most part I was a lone wolf in a pact of sheep dogs. I got bored more often than not.

I started to hang out at the library to pass the time and be out of Terri's hair on her time off. She loved me, but with the guys gone a lot and none of us "getting any" tensions were bound to get a bit higher. So I went off to seek refuge in this magnificent and I must say stunning library. Its huge windows looked out over the river that ran next to it. There was light honey colored wood everywhere that I loved. My favorite area had a couch and a couple of soft cushy chairs on which to sit my butt upon and contemplate what my next action in life should be. Getting a good job was top priority just my heart wasn't in it. No one other than Braiden was bugging me about the topic because I did what I could and helped out by cleaning and cooking the occasional meal.

I have learned at least twenty different ways to prepare and cook salmon. Salmon with cream cheese and raisin sandwiches were fast becoming my favorite. With Dad steadily sending some money I could give that to Terri to aid with our expenses. I am sure Braiden would prefer that I obtain a viable source of income. The first order of business when we arrived here in Ketchikan was to apply for food stamps. It really did get us through a rather tough time and I was grateful once I got past the stigma I had against it. There was some kind of pride issue involved as no one in my family ever had to be on assistance, not even the relatives who came through Ellis Island. Still it was a godsend for us to have a little extra to spend and so our trips to the local grocery were more pleasant. They had a Frogger game located near the ice machine so were able to get a few rounds in when we wee passing through.

By now the food stamps had long run out, but still we were managing. I was contributing in my own way by not being too much of a burden. It did little to ease my mind that I was somehow a failure by not working. Why did I resist work so much? I realized I was resisting a lot of things in my life. I did not want to grow up. Had little intention or desire of settling down any time soon or at any future date as far as I could tell.

Here in the library I could sit quietly for hours and wrestle with myself over issues and no one would bother me. I took up writing in a journal I had purchased much like one I kept in high school.

I wrote a little poem for Salmon, from the Salmons' point of view called "As I swim to spawn."

It goes like this:

Ode to a sickening human hand, oh here I wander lazily, through the never ending sea.
So, what is to become of me?
As I swim to spawn.
I whistle as I carelessly
make my journey up the stream. To help carry on my beautiful race, our scaly body so full of grace, and lets not forget our charming face.
As I swim to spawn.
But as a young one I learned in school, that our enemy, as a rule, was a human animal.
They are said to be floating above, over our calm water you see. Always hunting in our sea. So right now I fear for me.
As I swim to spawn.
Oh will I ever make it there? This swim seems so long and endless. So in these murky depths I swim. Hoping I go unnoticed. Remembering uncle Horas? And what our mothers told us.
As I swim to spawn.
My journey's end is coming near. I think I may escape the fear. And survive one more year. But sadly though no one knows if ill ever make the run again. I ponder on this thought a while, that at least I made it and I smile. Without getting caught by a fisherman.
As my goal is at its end. I am not mangled in a can. I think I am happy as a clam.
As I swim to spawn.

All right, I never claimed it was good, and my last name is nowhere near Browning" but I have no intention of making a living as a poet. It keeps me occupied though, and that's the main point.

When I get bored I am in the perfect surroundings to read the literature that surrounds me. All the classics surround me and of course the complete works of Jack London. The vision of Alaska that he puts forth in no way reflects what I have seen, but I highly doubt he was anywhere close to this place. I am sure he was further north. Still, his was a world of frozen harsh waste land, silence and desolation, a time when bars were called saloons and man held lofty ideas to get rich off gold mining. When hookers were plentiful and rules of living were being broken faster than they were being made.

The booze still flows freely up here and life can be tough if you're not prepared. This is the land where men are always and forever looking to get rich off something. Ever so often you can catch a glimpse of Alaska's bawdy past, hints that life was just a gun slinging rough and ready free for all. There were brothels that existed here in town that are long gone and now are just a tourist spot. I have yet to see a sled dog, let alone a sled.

Come to think of it there really aren't that many cats up here either. Currently in this day and age I would say that there is not even a struggle for survival in the elemental sense, it's more of a mental issue. Mr. London would probably be appalled at the lack of harshness. After all isn't that what everyone expects of Alaska. Mine is an unexpected interpretation of it all. Reading "Call of The Wild" while actually here in this library gives it an air of realism. And while I feel a connection and camaraderie with "Buck" I still have yet to find my inner wolf.

It was now three o'clock and time to get back to the apartment, Braiden would be getting home early and he and I and Terri and Zig would be kayaking over to Pennock Island to see his float house. It should be fun as I have never kayaked before. When

I arrived back at Terri's, Braiden had already made it home. We then all headed down to the dock, where two kayaks were.

"Oh my God, no way no fucking way am I getting in that! Its right on the water! It's in the water, the dark murky water! Hell no I won't go! (like I was a protester leftover from the hippie era). I am not getting in and you can't make me" I was having a small hissy fit. While Braiden was playing push me pull you with my left arm as I seamed to have grown spikes out of the bottom of my feet, because they were digging into the planks on the dock at this point.

It never dawned on me before that these wooden vessels I had seen in passing were what in fact what a kayak was. They are narrow and small and funny looking pointy boat things that you had to sit down in. There was nothing but an inch or so of wood, between you and hypothermia.

Braiden was smirking a little, but was firm and stated in a hushed tone. "Get in the kayak now, you have to get in, just get in, you're making a scene and people are staring. You'll be fine I swear, I'll have Zig take you and I'ill go over with Terri if that makes you feel better? Just get in."

To which I smiled and stated "You cant make me, I hate you" I was almost bratty, well I did spit and stomp my foot a little.

Just then Zig came over and calmed me down "Doris it will be fine, we do this all the time and no one has been lost in the water yet. I will take you across and you'll see it's no big deal. Okay?" Looking at him I saw that he exuded confidence and that nothing would happen, he was going to take care of me. So what could I do, I gave in.

The water as I said was dark, very dark almost black in its darkness, and still, like science fiction movie stillness where you know something is "Lurking" beneath waiting to tip over the flimsy kayak and devour you, leaving no trace. I am sure I held my breath the entire duration, it was not very far but which seemed like a one hundred mile trip. I knew in this water there were things that ate other things. I had seen all those movies where the thing under the water was watching just below the surface at the other things crossing over the water. As my imagination started to totally go wild, we had arrived at the float house and docked the blasted piece of boat like equipment.

Terri handed me a beer and I drank it like I had just crossed the Sahara. After a few minutes I remembered to breathe again and started to actually look around at how beautiful this place was. From this island, Ketchikan looked like somebody had painted it. And Pennock Island was serene and untouched and you could hear birds cawing and fish jumping and it was silent and calm.

The float house was eerily beautiful, built by Zig's own hands as he was a master craftsman. It perched up on stilts just off the shore of the island. The logs were a warm golden color and it was all in all the size of a decent living room, small kitchen, a bed and a closet. Is that all? Wait no bathroom? Then where do you…? Before I could ask, there was Braiden taking a leak off the back deck of the place. Then I don't want to know what happened if and when you needed to do the other bodily function. I never asked. Draw your own conclusions. I think there was a bucket by the door or something. Other than that it was romantic in its feel, with lots of pillows on the bed and a couple of woolen winter blankets.

You could imagine having a rendezvous with some married person here when discretion was in order. There was a small deck that wrapped all around it and the poles where we parked the kayaks. If you stood or sat on the little deck you could peer straight down into the water that was about two feet deep, very shallow, no threat, and lovely to look at. Fish were swimming and there were a couple of large crabs walking around down on the very bottom. Just resting on rocks were a few orange starfish, staring up at me, at least I think they were staring at me? Come to think of it I don't know that I have ever seen eyes on a starfish or even thought to look. I forgot where I was for a moment as I was one with the sea life and my companions were just happy I was calm, quiet and occupied.

"Look at the pretty fish and the big crabs!" I remarked like one of the toddlers we had seen at the aquarium.

"Yes they are nice, here have another beer!" Braiden handed me this next one and went back to the inside of the cabin to talk with Terri and Zig, while I sat and stared in the water. Float houses are fantastic of course because they offer freedom and privacy but their other plus was that the government can't tax them. I am sure they will find a way at a later date but right now they are tax free living at its best.

I could hear the conversation inside even though they believed they were whispering.

"So, Bray, how do you think she is really holding up? Terri and I have been a little concerned that this isn't the place for her? Maybe it was a bad idea and she needs to go home?" Zig was so sweet to be thinking of little ol' me.

"Hiccup" the second beer it seems was taking effect. "Burp!" did that come out of me I giggled "Scuse' me. "It's okay, you're excused"

Braiden shouted back jokingly. "Nah, she's fine, really, it's just a bit more overwhelming than she thought it was going to be, or I thought it would be. I guess we misjudged how tough it was to live up here. Anyway, this is her first real trip away from home. It's like the first time you go away to camp as a kid you just need a little time to adjust to it all. Really she'll be fine I am sure, in another couple of weeks everything will be fine." Braiden sounded like he was trying to convince himself as well as his brother that we could handle this. He did have a positive tone so what could I do but step up to the challenge and start to fit in better. Darn it! I was going to look harder at getting a job! Tomorrow! Not today, now it was time for one more beer!

"Can I have another beer pleeeeeease!" I asked all sweet and polite like, as I happened to lean to one side and peak into the open cabin door. And what do you know; one magically appeared at my side, along with Braiden as he came to sit with me.

"It's beautiful here, really beautiful, and the crabs, can I reach in and pick one up?" I dipped my hand into the water a bit and Braiden was quick to pull it out.

"I don't think that is such a good idea. Let's just sit here for a while." We sat and looked at the water and the living things in it, and it wasn't so scary anymore. I smiled and felt warm and lighter in spirit. Of course it could very well have been the beer but who am I to look a gift crab in the claw. The ride back in the kayak wasn't nearly as bad and I even let Braiden drive the one I was in.

The next morning I went out and procured a temporary job at the Stop Mart. I was just there to help out until I could find more lucrative employment with an advancement opportunity. Hey the pay was decent and it was a pleasant environment and it meant I would no longer be perceived as a free loading bum. So, life was good. When I got to Terri's' apartment after my shift at Stop Mart there was Braiden, and wow, Steve from the ferry, Zig and Terri, a really attractive young woman with blue eyes and long blonde hair, who I had not met before. She was probably a friend of Steve's and Val and her new boyfriend Eddie who is a hypnotist and who studied eastern healing practices. Terri and I had drinks with him and Val on Tuesday and their friend Bertram who was a rather well groomed man, which I believe is the only gay man in Alaska I imagine?

We lived a few doors away from an older gay couple in Alameda who had been together twenty years. They were classy and nice and there house was filled with antiques because that was what they did for a living, sell collectables and antiques. So Bertram was cool with me. He was a sculptor and artist and also made his own pasta, which I hope he brought some with him? There they all were in the living room.

"Well hello everyone, hi Steve, fancy meeting you here, and Eddie and Bertram nice to see you again. Are we having a party?"

I asked hoping that we were, because a joint would hit the spot right now. I cannot even recall when I last had one. Even with being unemployed I seemed to always be too occupied lately to stop and party. I felt pretty good but I find there's always room for improvement.

"Hi, Doris, you remember Steve from the ferry? Turns out he and Zig are old friends, and this is Kim, and you remember Bertram, and you have already met Eddie, Val's boyfriend." Braiden introduced us all formally. After a fine meal ,pasta my favorite. Bar-b-cued salmon and lots of red wine we were back in the living room. The weed seemed to appear out of nowhere and Val and Zig shared their collective stash of blow.

After the chit chat had died down Eddie became annoyed by what he felt was some tension in the air. "I feel some negative energy in the air, who hasn't had an aura cleansing lately?" Eddie asked. Of course I was the one who had not had one, and I am not sure what it was. I think he was making stuff up but I could be wrong? Braiden always said he could read auras and he tried once, but well, I remember how that went. I kind of knew what an aura reading was but to cleanse my aura? That sounded a bit iffy. Being the one ever to try new things and also a bit loaded off my ass I of course spoke up.

"Will this hurt? Do I leave my clothes on?" I asked reluctantly. "

No, just lay down on your back and you'll see, it feels really good, trust us." Terri said. But I got an eerie feeling anyway since people in horror films usually say things like that right before they sacrifice the virgin to the lava God. No chance of that happening here, no volcano and unless you can become a born again virgin, I knew it wasn't a sacrifice.

I laid down on my back and Braiden, Val, Terri and Eddie knelt around my body while Zig, Bertram, Steve, and Kim sat on the couch. I got the feeling they didn't know me well enough to be this intimate with me. I was on my back and they all began to rub their hands together then placing there hands about two to three inches above my body. Soon they began to make a sort of sweeping motion then they shook their hands away from me. Much the same motion as when your hands have fallen asleep and your trying to get circulation back. I was told to close my eyes and relax. As I did this I could feel heat from their hands all over me. After a good five minutes of this I was told to slowly open my eyelids and I must admit feeling an odd but pleasant sensation from some deeply spiritual place. I was helped up because I am pretty sure I would have passed out if left to do it alone.

"Braiden it's late could you give me a ride home?" The young and very shapely Kim asked. Braiden and his eyes seemed to widen a little, so I chimed in.

"I'll go with you I would love to take a little ride out in the cool evening air." I felt it curious that Kim asked Braiden to take her home; I thought she was a close friend of Steve's? No matter, there we were all crammed in the front seat of the cab; I sat in between Braiden and Kim because she was getting out. Braiden brought home the "Crab Cab" because he was doing a split shift. We stopped in front of her apartment without Braiden ever asking her for directions, and Braiden got out and helped open the car door for Kim.

"It was nice to meet you Kim." I yelled out the window of the cab. The cool wind on my warm flushed cheeks felt refreshing, and watched him walk her up the stairs to her door. Although they were out of earshot I saw Kim touch his shoulder, and slip Braiden something that he then put in his pocket, and then he pulled something out of his pocket and gave it to her. Just at that moment they both glanced over at me for some reason smiled and waved. I managed a weak wave back. Then they looked in each other's eyes mumbled something inaudible to each other and shook hands like old pals would.

Braiden got back in the car and I was falling asleep at this point so I could only get out a few words " That was nice of you to drive her home and see here to her door, you must be psychic because you did not even ask her for directions. She is a very attractive young lady, don't you think so? I thought she was with Steve? It was interesting to see Steve again. He's seems like such a nice guy, I like him. Have you met Kim before? I haven't seen her around before. I thought I had met every one in this already. What did you two exchange, phone numbers? I bet you wish, I hadn't driven her home with you, wink, wink." I nudged him gently and jokingly in the arm. To which he replied.

"Yes, she is very pretty, and I have given her a few rides in the cab. Strictly business that's all. Picked her up from the store, and "The Shipwreck" bar a couple of times, but that's all. I gave her a match, she was out and she wanted a cigarette. She gave me five bucks because one time she stiffed me on a tip. That's all. And yes, Steve is very nice and I guess it was odd seeing him tonight. Now I have to drop you back at Terri's before I go start my second shift.

We were now only a few blocks from home and although the whole thing with Kim seemed rather odd, I was too tired and feeling way too mellow to care to find out anything more. I had suspicions but they would just have to wait until a more appropriate time. Braiden helped me up the stairs and into bed, taking off my shoes for me and throwing a comforter over my body.

"Hey, you wanna fool around?" I asked grabbing at his shirt.

"No, not now, I don't have time. I have to get to work. Tomorrow is my day off and we can spend the day together if you like." I nodded into my pillow and let the wave of sleep wash over me.

CHAPTER TWELVE
The State Bird of Alaska is the Salmon...

I was getting really good at kayaking now and was getting in shape .I could make it back and forth to Pennock in record time and on my own when I felt like it. Someone was always kind enough to lend me a kayak or anything else for that matter. The people up here are all sweet and gentle, and have been very nice to me. I would go so far as to say that they make people back home appear uncivilized and unfriendly. I took one kayak trip with Eddie because I wanted the practice. It turned out to be a short trip because he mentioned to me how we could make out by Snows Cove and no one would ever know. Well wrong, I would know! So, taking charge I pointed our kayak back to the mainland and docked it in record time.

There had been some talk in town about a rather large yacht that was parked in the cove by Zigs' float house. It had somehow mysteriously appeared in the morning. No one heard any noise or saw anything, but there it was in all its white majestic glory. Braiden and I were on a mission to find out who the mystery yacht owner was. We owed it to all the townsfolk to investigate.

At 11pm on a very dark night with clouds covering the moon and black water below we went to investigate. The water did not bother me so much any longer as I now knew I could fall in and die of hypothermia before anything would eat me alive. That was a comforting thought. We approached the cove and slowly turned the kayak. This thing was massive and white and looked out of place. We stopped about fifty feet from it, close enough to see in but far enough to high tail it out in case someone came out on deck with guns blazing. We stared at it in awe and I could see into a living room of sorts with, get this, crystal chandelier. Shit! Come on, who does this over the top and rich boat, belong to? Some famous names were tossed around in the bar we were at earlier, but I really did not see anyone to confirm any of the rumors. It struck me that it could also be a drug dealer or someone with some shady dealings to own a yacht that looked this attractive. It was quiet as we peered and pondered, no one was visible at the time. Until two rather large and unfriendly Dobermans came on deck and proceeded to bark incessantly.

"Bray, can Doberman's, swim?" I asked not really wanting a response. I figured it was time to end the expedition and high tail it back to the main land. Pronto! Braiden felt this was a good decision as well, and followed my lead in turning the kayak around. At that precise moment a male figure appeared on deck to see what the dogs were barking at. I did not stay to stare and try to find out who it actually was. I at this point, did not care.

The day next day came and so did the end to my loafing. Braiden had had enough, and on this cold and damp morning I was forced to apply for work on the dreaded slime line at the Mistress of the Water Cannery. I lost my little job at the Snack Fast Shop Mart. I was let go because business was slow and she couldn't afford to pay me. That was days ago and Braiden had no intention of letting my unemployment drag on as long as it did before. So here we were on our way to the dreaded cannery.

"Hell No I won't go!!!" I protested in the cab as he drove. "No you can't make me do this, I won't do it! It's not fair! I have rights! I will find a lawyer. I promise I will start looking again for a job, we're doing okay, I hate you." he said not a word until he parked the car and pulled me out literally kicking and screaming like a toddler on his reluctant first day of school.

"It won't be that bad, you'll make friends and you'll gut some fish. It will be an adventure, you'll be fine. It will be fun. You'll see." He said smiling and sort of laughing like this was a joke. It seemed all too sinister to me.

"Hell, no I'm not going I'm not I'm not, I hate you! I hate you! And I never want to see you again, I'll get on the next plane out of here, I swear to God if you make me go in there!" I started to hyperventilate a little.

Braiden dragged me up to a group of people and started to introduce me "This is Doris and she is going to work with you guys today. Could you look after her until I pick her up at 5.?" They said "Sure" in polite unison. I got the feeling they felt I was in need of some gentle reassurance, and possibly some medication.

One of the young women grabbed my shoulders in an attempt to comfort me. "You'll be fine here, I'm Sandra. Your okay now, we have all felt a little apprehensive at first about working here. It's really hard work but once you get the hang of it, well, the time just flies by. Tammy over here has worked here for seven years now right Tammy?" Tammy gave a nod. Sandra continued "Just give it a try first; you'll see it's not that bad! Okay?"

At hearing this news I was less than reassured. In fact, I was freaking me out even more hearing this woman had been working here for seven years, my gawd!!! What is wrong with you people? Maybe if I run off into the woods and hide, they will all leave me alone? Run! The voice in my head said Run! Before you become one of them!

Instead in a rather weak and quiet outward voice I replied, "Oh, okay" then for the better part of the morning barely said anything to anyone. I was put on the slime line and left alone probably due to the crazed look in my eyes and the seven-inch blade I was given to gut the fish with.

Let me explain a "Slime Line." You are given a white coat and a large knife. I mean a very large knife; it looked like the kind you would need to cut a path through jungle brush. You are placed in a line with a few other people near a long conveyor belt. It has a small stream of water that runs through it and then it starts. Here come the salmon in all their scaly glory. You are informed and time has returned me to the present moment of living hell of which I am currently involved in. Ah! I am thrown back into the harsh reality, as scales are in fact flying up and attaching themselves to my face. Much as I would imagine barnacles do to a slow moving whale. The monotony of the conveyor belt is excessive to say the least. Inserting the knife gives an evil sort of pleasure as it is inserted. To slice from one end of their body to the other is sadistic in nature. This is with one hand, with the other hand you stick your fingers in and in one swoop you pull all the guts out. Right hand knife slash, left hand, clean sweep of insides.

I had gone into mental overdrive mechanically performing my duty up until five 'o'clock when the whistle blew, yep there was a whistle, just like in the "Flintstones" cartoon when Fred yells "Yabba Dabba Do!!!" Except I didn't much feel like letting out any "Yabba" let alone any "Dabba Do" at this moment. Maybe later after a very long hot shower, consisting of a gallon of soap and shampoo and perfume and after I burn these clothes! Then a few beers, and maybe after that I may "Yabba Do". Not before though. No, not now. Now I said bid farewell to my new chum buddies.They were nice enough folks and I may see them around the town but I will not be returning to this place. I hung up my smock, collected my day's wages of $120. Shit, the money was fantastic but the job sucked fish eggs! Literally. I still had no intention of coming back. The money I earned should be enough to keep Braiden off my back but I am getting other employment! In the morning! Even if I have to drive a cab along side him.

I opened the heavy steel door that led from inside to civilization again. The cold air pushed at my back, and I felt the warm sun hit my face. It was bright! I had to squint. I almost forgot what the outside world was like while I was doing time here in fish prison. I will now probably have to get some sort of tattoo in order to commemorate my term of employment incarceration. For some weird reason I felt an urge to have a cigarette? I dragged my exhausted, fatigued body and broken spirit to the taxi where Braiden was waiting. I wondered if I should speak to him at all. I didn't feel much like conversation. He of course would be cheerful because all he had to do was sit on his bony ass, and drive tourists around all day. Big fucking whoop! Poor baby!

I could barely lift the door handle to get in while Braiden stayed behind the wheel waiting for me. I literally slid into the seat like a de-boned chicken. It felt good to sit down. My head went back onto the headrest and then dropped over to look at Braiden who at this point was staring at me mortified.

"Honey, you have "things" on your face? Should I wipe them off?" he asked cautiously like you would to a serial killer whose still holding the meat hook.

"They're scales! NO! Don't touch them! They can't be wiped off! I'll get a hideous rash and I'll be disfigured for life!!!! " I snapped! Then I just started crying and Braiden got all gentle and tried to hug me. "No! Don't hug me or you'll get them on you too!" I screeched.

He patted me on the shoulder and apologized profusely in a nervous laughing kind of way. "I am soooo sorry, please forgive me, I had no idea it would be that difficult I thought they would give you office work or something? I was wrong, we'll go home you get cleaned up and then we will go out to eat, you pick the place? Would you like that?" I nodded as I continued to sob all the way home. He got us back to the apartment in record time.

Terri was at the door and looked at me in total pity and shock, "What happened to you sweetie?" she said as she tried to hug me, and I ran crying into the bathroom. "Braiden what happened? What did you do to her?" Terri asked.

"Oh, I dropped her at the cannery to get hired on. It was

horrible from what I could understand. She tried to explain on the way home but there was all this crying going on."

"Oh, Braiden you shouldn't have done that, not her! How could you?" she was a little pissed.

"I know that now, I feel bad enough." He sighed as I shut the bathroom door and stayed in there cowering and cleaning myself like a wounded animal for well over an hour. The first ten minutes of which I was in there I just stared at my disheveled self in the mirror .I emerged from the bathroom slowly and timidly as I had seen small animals do on National Geographic, when they come out of the ground to smell the air for safety. It seemed non-threatening enough now. I was less messed up than when I went in but still a little shaky. I needed food and a drink and merriment and lots of reassurance that I never had to go back there again. Okay, deep breath, let it out, okay exhaling is good. Braiden and Terri were sitting on the couch facing the door as I came out. I think they had sat there for the duration I was in the bathroom.

"Are you feeling better?" Terri asked first.

Then Braiden said "Yeah honey, are you ready to go get some food now? Would you like that?" I nodded with a halfhearted smile on my face. It would just be Braiden and I for dinner, even though I wanted Terri to come with us, she had some things she to do. She wanted us to come home for dessert because she had made a chocolate cake and thought it would make me feel better. We agreed and headed out to "The Grizzly House." One of the best restaurants in town of which there were only two best restaurants. The other one was the "Velvet Moose" ah, yep! It was much more expensive.

We arrived at The Grizzly to find that Kim would be our waitress. I still figured something was up between Braiden and her but I had only speculation to go on. She seemed pleasant enough; I still wished Steve was her boyfriend. Maybe I can nudge her into that concept. Steve is a nice guy and he does own part of the fishing boat that Zig went out on. I recently learned from Val that Kim came from Reno Nevada and had followed her then boyfriend up here two years ago. They have since broken up and he went back to Reno. Oddly enough she grew to like it here so much she stayed.

Well, this was her job, small world. "Hey Braiden and Doris, good to see you, are you dining here tonight or just going to the bar?" she said with her happy blue eyes flashing.

"We are eating here tonight Kim, for a treat. We don't have a reservation. Can you squeeze us in?" Braiden asked in a way that how could she refuse.

"Sure! Of course right this way!" she seated us even though it was not her job. She explained they were short handed that one of the waitresses had just quit so they had to replace her. The hostess was out sick tonight. Luckily it was slow so while we looked over the menu Kim chatted with us. "Doris how's the job hunting going, have you found anything yet?"

"No, not much, I have been doing some work here and there and Braiden did his part in my quest for work today by dropping me off at the cannery where I was forced to do hard labor by breaking rocks with a sledge hammer and work the slime line but other than that not much" I spoke into my menu.

"Icck! Oh my God Braiden how could you! "Imagine that, Kim was on my side. "Listen, Doris would you like to try out as a waitress? I know I could get you on here The owner is a real sweetheart of an old man named Henry Brinkleman .In fact he is here right now, I am going to go talk to him and have him come over to meet you. Hang on I'll be right back."

Before I could protest, not that I would, she was off and away. She was back five minutes later with a man I presumed to be Henry right behind her.

"Hello my dear, I am Henry. Can you start tomorrow night? About 5pm?" I guess he made up his mind? I don't know what Kim said but bless her for it.

"Sure sir yes, I can do that. You should know I have never

waited tables before?" I was thinking I am so glad I cleaned myself up.

"That's fine Kim will teach you everything you need to know. I will see you tomorrow so enjoy your meal on me tonight. "He shook Braiden's' hand and then my own and I guess the deal was done I was now employed.

I would no longer have to consider stripping at the "The Funky Penguin," or even reopening what I liked to call the "Flop and Screw" the infamous brothel and hotel down near the docks that had closed down. Our conversation lagged but our meal was lovely. I had a pasta dish and Braiden had a pork chop.

"Well gee Bray are you happy now I that I have employment?" I asked taking a heaping spoonful of ice cream sundae into my mouth.

"Yes, I suppose I am. Are you going to make this one work now? It would really take the stress off me in trying to support us both." Braiden had a snotty tone to his reply but I felt he was justified.

"I not only intend to make this job a success for me but I am going to change my entire life and be the pillar of a model citizen. Now do you want to go home and have some sex or what?" I figured it was worth a shot to ask.

"Look, I am not quite sure what kind of role model you're going to be, and for that matter to who. But yeah, I could go for some sex. And this time let's try to relax a little." After we finished dessert we headed home and within a half hour we were in bed. I intended do my best tonight to make things between us stayed as steamy as they used to be. Terri and Zig were out but a note to eat some of the chocolate cake that she baked.

We lit some candles, dimmed the lights, pulled back the bedspread and blankets, and put the radio on some quiet jazzy station. I lay back on the bed and watched Braiden take off his shirt and unzip his pants.

I got up and took off my blouse and had a rather naughty idea. "Bray would you care for some cake?" I said.

"Well, ah, no not right now. Didn't you get enough dessert at the restaurant?" He replied because he wasn't sure where it was all leading.

"I always have room for more sweets. I would like some cake and I think you actually do too." I went into the kitchen and hacked off a large chunk of cake and brought it back, wrapped in a napkin. I locked the door behind me, and placed the cake down on the nightstand while Braiden lay on the bed with only the glow of the candle light covering him. I slowly removed the rest of my clothing and grabbed a handful of cake and smeared it onto Braiden's chest and stomach. He had a surprised but pleased look across his face as he now understood where all this was going. He knelt up on the bed and followed my lead. The next forty-five minutes were filled with a flurry of hands and cake and tongues and kisses and activities that ultimately ended in a satisfied sharing of body, soul, spirit and a little weed.

Whatever was bothering him before had not reared its head this day, nothing got in the way. Our relationship as far as I was concerned, at least the physical part, was back to the way it was.

The next morning I had a job to go to, I was employed. Yippee! I now had a real job. I felt much like Pinocchio felt when he became a real boy. Except I had not turned into a real boy I had turned into a waitress and a barmaid.

It took me about a week to get the hang of it. My first day way grueling and I got a few orders wrong but eventually it got easier. The money and tips were great, but the best part was I made friends easily and instantly. Finally it had seemed I found something I was good at and happy to do for a living. Working here also came with the perk of getting a meal on your shift. I ate very well and the food was tasty and hanging out after my shift was just as wonderful. I would get a drink at the bar and chat with all my new buddies.

As time progressed I found myself getting home later than Braiden. Who by now, was back working days and only one shift, because I was bringing home ample cash to help out. However

Braiden was back to being displeased for some reason. Maybe now I had gone too far the other way and enjoyed my work too much. That would be a silly thing to get mad at. Wouldn't it?

Recently I had been learning how to barmaid and I was once asked for an "Orgasm" by one of the fisherman known by the name of "Butch." I kid you not, he was a regular patron. Not knowing at the time that an "Orgasm" was a fancy drink, I hauled off and slapped him. Luckily he and his buddies laughed and did not press assault charges because he thought I was cute. And he was three times my size. I paid for a round of drinks for him and his buddies and all was forgiven. He tipped me well every time after that that he came in.

This evening I managed to make it home in time to see that Braiden, Val, Zig and Terri were all in the living room. Wine glasses in hand and preoccupied looks on their faces.

"Hi everybody, what's up?" I used my concerned voice.

"Val and Eddie just broke up." Terri said and went to the kitchen.

"I am sorry to hear that. You are too good for him anyway. Is there anything I can do to help cheer you up?" I asked as Terri handed me my own glass of burgundy and sat on the floor.

"What could you possibly do?" Braiden answered in a snippy sort of way. His tone threw me off guard and so I sipped my drink and stayed on the floor, while the rest of them talked it out.

When the clock was coming up on eleven Val thought it wise to head on home. "Hey look it's getting late and I am tired and buzzed, I think I will head home now." Val remarked.

"Oh, hey I will drive you home, you're not in any condition to walk there on your own." Braiden seemed so gallant coming to his dear sisters side like this, but why was he so anxious to get out?

"Bray, I am perfectly fine I can make it home." Val was skeptical of his actions as well.

"No I insist." And they were out the door. I said my good

nights crawled into bed and had no need to count sheep as my head hit the pillow. Braiden must have come in later but I was out cold, exhausted from another honest days work, smiling to myself as my eyes closed. I heard him quietly shut the door, the clinking of his belt being undone and the woosh of his pants falling to the floor. I felt the covers being pulled back and the sag of the mattress as he crawled in. I was deep in dreamy state but I snuggled up next to him to cuddle and he just rolled over turning away from me.

"Bray, is their something the matter? Do you want to talk? Why are you acting so cold towards me? Did I do something wrong?' I was groggy but somewhat coherent.

"I don't think we need to get into this now, just go to sleep. It's late too late just go to sleep." He said. What did he mean by too late? Did he mean too late to talk? Or, could it be too late for us? Either way it probably meant I would now be having nightmares mixed in with troubling thoughts of impending doom. Why didn't he have the decency to lie to me until the morning so I could have slept well and awoke refreshed? Then I would be ready to talk, shit there he slept now, while I was wide awake pondering all variations of disaster that await me.

CHAPTER THIRTEEN

"Have another drink, don't mind if I do!"

I awoke this morning with an unpleasant feeling in my gut, perfectly understandable as the last few nights it's been rather chilly in the bedroom. I had caught an emotional flu. Because I was resilient enough to get past all that, I should be feeling great. It was the beginning of July and that meant a Fourth of July celebration was on its way.

In another week I would be turning the big two-oh! I already have been drinking alcohol legally while up here, because the legal age is nineteen. If I ever head back to California I still had another birthday to get through before I could drink legally there. I am not sure how that would change anything I was already partaking in it legal or not.

It makes no sense that you can go to war at the age of eighteen, fight, defend and die for your country, get a job and live on your own, give birth to children and be a parent at any age after hitting puberty. If you get a note from your parents you can own a firearm. But you cannot drink alcohol? So, in effect you are able to create these problems in your life but are not yet old enough to drink to forget them. In my opinion this is totally illogical.

What was bothering me? Oh yes, now I recall. Aside from

whatever was going on between me and Braiden. It was also the day that Susie our hostess at "The Grizzly" was leaving to head back home to Utah to get ready for her upcoming entrance into college. All of us waitresses and waiters alike were crossing our fingers that we would get the promotion that her leaving opened up. I really wanted this position, everyone did. It was the best position in the whole damn place. You get to wear nice clothing and you don't have to serve anyone. At the end of the day you don't smell like whatever was the special of the day at the end of the night. No perspiration. On top of all that the waiters and waitresses have to share their tips with you. Life was truly lopsided. I had not been doing all that well at work. Lately I was poorly tipped even though I was courteous.

I was getting a reputation for being a tough broad on the job. When I saw Dan the sweaty, short and round busboy steal one of my tips I cornered him in the kitchen and hit him repeatedly with my serving tray over and over again until Henry the manager stopped me. I got my ass pinched at least twice every night in the first few days I was there. On the third day I grabbed one of the pinchers hand and bent his wrist back so far he screamed.

In spite of all this I really truly liked my job. The food was great and I adored most of my co-workers. I had made lots of friends and I was paid a decent wage for doing honest work. I was determined to keep it whether or not I was chosen for the hostess gig.

My shift that day was rough, I got an order wrong had a drink spilled on me by accident and lost one of my earrings. Before I finished my shift there was a small going away ceremony for Susie with cake and we were informed who would replace her. I held my breath in anticipation. It was, Deidre. Oh, well, she was a nice enough person, she worked hard and as much as I was hoping it was me, I was glad that someone got it that actually deserved it. I congratulated her and felt the right choice had been made. Then I headed for home.

I decided not to call Braiden to pick me up. A walk is what

I needed on this day. I would call him to meet me at our hang out the "The Pasta Tree". It was about a mile and a half away. As I walked I buttoned down my collar and unbuttoned my black velvet work vest. Then, off came my name-tag, and down came my hair.

I realized the sun was shining and the warmth on my face felt good. Up here the sun comes out on rare occasions, its usually cloudy and rains about 298 days out of the year. The sun is a treasured commodity and when it does come out everyone strips off their clothing and runs wild in the streets. Well not really, but in my twisted imagination they do. Life is sweet when it's sunny and people smile more and dealing with challenges gets put in better perspective, until it starts to rain again.

But the weather was not the sole reason for why my spirits felt lifted. Things were in fact looking up, regardless of the fact that Deidre got the job. I felt strong and self sufficient for the first time in my pathetic little life. I let out a deep sigh and noticed I felt pretty good. I thought I would be more disappointed. It dawned on me that with that position came more commitment and more responsibility than I really wanted to put in. So it was a good thing. I was intent on keeping this job because if I didn't it was back to the slime line. I had not yet totally given up the stripping idea, as either one are basically the same job, performing a nasty and dirty task while being slightly demeaned.

With my backpack slung over my shoulder I stopped into the Shipwreck bar. I ordered a big glass of orange juice and to said hello to my friends there, namely Joe the bartender. His family owned half the town and I felt he may have some advice or know of an apartment Braiden and I could rent. Even though we had discussed it days ago I felt that moving out on our own was still part of the plan. It was getting pretty crowded over at Terris' because Zig decided to have an extended stay with her before he went out on one of the fishing boats again.

The Shipwreck was one of the more splendid bars, it even had its own T-shirts and you could buy one for $12.50. Somehow I never felt the burning desire to own one. Nice T-shirt though, it was of a drunk guy with an eye patch and parrot on his shoulder passed out on the bar, with a fruity looking drink in hand that included the tiny umbrella. Looking at it would conjure up some odd questions. Can a pirate can actually drink that much? And why doesn't his parrot fall off? First off, wouldn't a pirate have built up some sort of alcohol immunity? And what's with the fruity drink? I was under the impression that pirates imbibed only in rum? Second, about this parrot, I would hope some sort of animal protection agency would take it away from him? It was a fun picture though. I think this bar was one of the first ever built up here?

"Afternoon Joe, how are you doing? Lovely day isn't it?" I was almost surprised at how cheery I sounded, oh well.

"Hello my dear Doris, it is a splendid day and I am fine. How are you? Can I pour you a glass of something?" Joe asked smiling, and I of course got my orange juice on the house. I would crinkle my nose at him and he seemed to like this and it made him happy and for a free glass of orange juice I was pleased to accommodate him.

"Joe, Braiden and I are starting to look for a place of our own to rent. Do you know of any one bedroom apartments for about $800 or so?

Joe said he did not know of any rentals but would keep an ear out for me. For me anything! After a chat and when my glass was empty I said goodbye and continued on my merry little way. I swear if I knew how to whistle I would be doing it now. I just felt light and had that spring in my step. You know the one we always hear happens when you feel just happy for no particular reason.

I arrived at the Pasta Tree and I called Braiden at "the Crab Cab" to come pick me up. He was getting off at six anyway so while I was going to wait might I might as well feed my tummy with some tasty spaghetti and one of their wonderful pineapple shakes. They were heaven! This was a lovely day.

I hope the weather holds out for the parade tomorrow, as it's the fourth of July. I had just finished eating my last bite of spaghetti when Braiden showed up to take me home. I wanted to stay in this evening and go to bed early so I would enjoy the Fourth of July festivities. As much as I didn't want to ruin my happy feeling I knew this was the ideal time to talk to Bray and finally clear up some of the issues we were having, whatever those might be. I was apprehensive but took a deep breath and while Braiden looked straight ahead to drive I spoke as calmly as was possible.

"Bray, I feel we have not been connecting very well lately, what's going on? I thought for a while things were getting better between us and now the only thing I am sure about is that I'm confused. Do you want to talk to me?" There, I said it. I put it all out on the table and it was his turn to come clean and clear the air. I watched him drive.

The sun came through the windshield, shining on his golden brown hair, looking a little tired but still as attractive as always, but different somehow? Was it a change in his looks? Or was the change coming from somewhere deeper inside him? I wasn't able to tell.

"I am a little worn out from work, living up here, being with you and all the responsibility I now have .Having to play adult wears on me sometimes. It's way more intense than I anticipated." He said, then sighed but seemed a bit relieved to say it out loud. I imagine it has been playing on his mind for days now maybe weeks.

"I understand, I know what you mean. Look at me. I have steady employment and I am almost respectable. It freaks me out sometimes. But I am kind of digging it as I saw a smile creep over his face and I was feeling a bit more relaxed.

"Hey, I spoke to Joe today on my way to "The Pasta Tree" and I asked him if he knew of any rentals in our price range. He didn't know of any but said he would keep let me know if he heard of any. You still wanted to get an apartment, right? I mean with me of course? We are still an item aren't we?"

At this he glanced at me briefly with raised eyebrow. "Yes, I think we should move into our own place and yes as far as I can tell we are still together. What kind of a question is that?" by this time we were pulling up in front of Terri's so our heavy conversation had to come to a close. I was satisfied with our talk and it swept away some of my doubts. But only some of them, I was not ready to delve any deeper into my other suspicions of him and Kim and how much interaction might be going on between them.

For the Fourth of July parade a lively crowd of about twelve hundred gathered early. That was a large turn out considering the rest of the town was the actual parade. It wasn't fancy, but made up for it with unbridled enthusiasm. They had boated in two horses from Prince Rupert for the occasion, a small band passed by and then several cars, about seven of them. Then it was the fire department and police cars followed behind. Just as it began quickly it ended even quicker.

"Whose up for some pancakes?" Zig asked.

"I'm in" Braiden replied first then Terri's "Me to" followed by my "You don't have to ask me twice. Who's cooking?" Later that night I decided I wanted to see the fireworks from the breakers. It was growing dark and almost time so I headed onto them with Braiden and others right behind me. No one was ever supposed to be out on this cement wall but it was dark and it was just this time. The national anthem blared from out of nowhere and then a barge appeared first it sprayed water then fireworks jumped out in all directions. It was truly the most simple and effective use of fireworks I had ever witnessed.

I must say I slept well that night, all cozy in the bed and curled up next to Braiden, very contented I might add. He and I were both off of work on the same day. So after Terri went off to her shop we ate breakfast and went back to bed. It was a lovely morning and afternoon because we ate lunch and then you guessed it, went back to bed.

For the next few days that followed we just worked and I must say we worked long and hard. I was getting a little worn out and for some odd reason a little homesick, although I really wasn't exactly sure, why?

There was some reason I felt oddly off center. Maybe it was that I am working too much? Or it could be that I had now fallen into a routine of work and then it was always a few drinks,a few rounds of pool or Ms Pac-Man, which I was getting good at. I felt old and hey? Wait a minute the reason I felt old was because my twentieth birthday was tomorrow! Shit! I am not even going to say anything, I am not going to remind anyone, and I will not make a big deal about it. It will be strictly business as usual, that's it.

I am going to buy myself something nice and I believe a drink or two will be in order. Maybe I'll ask Janis if she'll join me. I had better get all the legal booze I can handle so I can make it through the next year to twenty-one. That means I will get to celebrate being legal all over again. Whooo-hooo!

The sun rose in the sky, again. I got up and had coffee like I always do and read the paper. I have adopted the habit of turning on the radio while I read the paper and have my coffee and usually there is some hokey music playing. This morning was no exception it was a peppy little number called "Don't fence me in." The lyrics are "Give me land lots of land with the starry skies above." I know it's the universe trying to send me some sort of message but I just don't have the patience to figure it out right now. I have heard very little, if any, of the type of music I like to listen to. Funny thing is I hardly miss it. Braiden was already up and gone. I don't recall getting even a peck on the cheek this morning. Terri was at her shop already and I was all by my lonesome. Do I want to go shopping for my gift before I go work my shift, or after? Hum? Decisions, decisions.

I was working the lunch shift, which is short and right in

the middle of the day so it goes by fairly quickly but also breaks the whole day into two parts. I finally chose to go buy myself something after my shift because then I could take my time and not feel rushed. It just made more sense. My light birthday morning meal consisting of toast with salmon and cream cheese and a few raisins along with a chocolate chip cookie, after all it was my birthday. I got dressed for work in a hurry because I took an extra long shower and out the door I went. I worked my entire shift with my blouse inside out and no one said word one about it. Was anyone paying attention to me today? I broke a nail, I dropped a tray, and then my paycheck was short by twenty bucks. It was not exactly the day I had hoped for. It wasn't even close. Any other day would have been a day I could shrug it off but it bugged me today. Finally it was over I was released for the rest of the blasted afternoon.

"Good-Bye Everyone" I said as I started to take my vest off and head out the front door.

"Doris, wait you got a phone call, Braiden is on the phone" Jeff caught me two steps from the outside world, I was almost free, I could smell the air. Oh well.

"Hi Honey" I spoke with an air of irritation "Hi, I can't pick you up right now, you're going to have to walk. Can you meet me at five thirty at Northern Taco, you know that Mexican restaurant we went to before, do you remember?"

What could I say, how else could I reply, because this is how my day was going.

"Sure, no problem. Yes I remember the restaurant, see you later, Bye" then I headed out. I thought to myself, well at least he'll probably buy me dinner and a beer, so that was a good thing.

I had wanted this necklace for weeks now, it was a little gold crab made out of a gold nugget and he held in his little claws a small diamond. I had mentioned to Braiden I that I was going to save up for it. It cost around two hundred and seventy five dollars. I had paid off all my half of this months living expenses so I figured now was a good time to treat myself, my sorry little pathetic birthday self.

I walked in and looked at where it should have been, but it was missing. "Excuse me, do you know where the little crab necklace went?" I asked knowing full well it had to have been sold and probably to some stupid tourist just passing through. I imagined that she would buy it, wear it once and throw it in her jewelry box along side of her Puka shell necklace and her King-Tut souvenir commemorative ring.

"I am sorry it's been sold, I do have a nice dolphin if you want to look at it?" he was trying to be helpful but I snapped at him anyway.

"Dolphin, dolphin I don't want a dolphin. I am a crab, I wanted the crab." I had my hissy fit and left. Off to the Shipwreck to have a beer, or two so I could cry into them. Thank God for Joe, he listened to the full account of my awful day and my drinks were on the house. I was on my third one when I remembered I had to meet Braiden. I was feeling good real good and sort of slid off my bar stool very much like gelatin would if it had legs made out of fur, until my feet found the floor.

"Doris do you want me to get you a ride home?" Joe was a little concerned "Oh, Nooooooo Joe, I will be just hunky dory, I am meeting Braiden at the Mexican restaurant around the corner, I'm fine o'rooney!" Did I sound coherent?

It was about five forty five so I would be arriving just fine. Except it was Six forty five. I had read the clock wrong and I arrived to Braiden having his own version of a hissy fit, as I walked or should I say poured into the door.

"Doris, where the hell have you been, I was getting worried but thought maybe you had stopped by, hey you smell like beer how many did you have?"

"Its okay, I was with Joe and he took care of me really, really well, and now I am here, so feed me dinner." I did not slur that was a good sign. I was being led to a big table filled with all these people that we knew. Zig and Terri and Kim and Steve and Braiden's parents, oh hello!!!

"Bray, do you know your parents are here? Are they really here, do you see them too?" I asked.

"Yes I see them yes they are here to surprise you, SURPRISE and happy twentieth birthday" every one in the restaurant yelled surprise and I almost puked. A surprise party for me! The big surprise was that Braiden's' parents were here. Wow, and I got to sit right next to them, lucky me.

"How have you been my dear, happy birthday" I got a big awkward hug from Braiden's' Mom then his Dad.

"Good to see you. Mr., and Mrs., Host, Hostel teller, no that's not right?" Braiden chimed in with "Hostetler!" I said bless you like it was a sneeze and then I laughed and finished my sentence. "Yeah! Thanks for being here."

"So, my dear Doris how are you doing here? Are you well? Braiden was a little concerned about your adjusting to this sort of life and wanted us to come up and lend our support. And of course we were already coming up to comfort Val on her recent,(she whispered to me) breakup. " Mrs. Hostetler spoke in an odd motherly tone.

"Mrs. H, I am pretty sure Val knows she broke up with her boyfriend, she is sitting right next to you so you don't have to whisper. As for me, well, I had been wrestling with going back home now or staying here through the winter. You know that old saying "Catch as Ketchikan" I said and then I laughed and got a big kick out of myself. As everyone around the table followed my lead and laughed because it was my birthday and I was the guest of honor and then they went back to ordering food.

I was however corrected by Braiden in his serious voice because he was pissed that I was so late getting here. "No, that's not a saying it's a wrestling term, and it's Catch as Catch Can" it means "to grab hold anywhere your able."

So I replied in my witty and totally three sheets to the wind voice " Well that sounds appropo! Doesn't it?"

"So, how is Oscar? He was going to come up and visit me, ah, us he said he would? Haven't heard from him lately?" I asked in my most chit chatty type of speech.

"Oh, um didn't Braiden tell you? Oscar died of an overdose, or some bad heroine? It was something, along those lines. Can't really recall the details? We told Braiden in our last letter; wonder why he didn't tell you?" Mrs. Hostetler tried to sound matter of fact.

Inside my heart sank and I felt a lump of true sadness arise in my throat and I felt the bile enter up from my stomach but now was not the time. I would have to remind myself later to say a short prayer for this truly free spirit, to me Oscar will always be one magnificent creature, never truly appreciated on this earth. A being I would have very much liked to have known more about, now that would never happen.

"Oh, I guess he really had a bigger problem than I imagined? No, Bray never said anything to me about that. Not one lousy stinking word about it. " It was not a good time to cry. So I held myself back.

"Sorry, must have slipped my mind. Let's say we have a toast to Doris on being the tender and wise age of twenty." Braiden changed the subject which I felt for him was maybe a sore one.

"Here, Here. To Doris and many more" the table of people said almost in the same tone. Maybe he just didn't want to know how upset I would be at the news of Oscars passing. This thought somehow unnerved me, as Braiden was not a jealous sort? Or was he? I could never tell.

CHAPTER FOURTEEN
"Contemplation"

The people who study salmon tell us that there are many different types of the fish. Such as Coho, King or Chinook, Chum or Dog fish, Sockeye and Pink or hump, and maybe one or two other? It could be I think there are more because each type can be called by a couple different names, there is also much lingering debate of weather Trout is also a form or species of salmon. Salmon are born in fresh water and return to the ocean salt waters to mature, some may grow some odd looking teeth, or even a hump. I think they live about three to five years on average? Although, I am not one hundred percent on this, so don't quote me. On their final return trip to spawn, they die within a matter of a few days.

Before Braiden's' parents headed for home, we went out for a day trip to the place where the salmon swim up stream to spawn. The sight was frightening; the seagulls were taunting and picking at the poor struggling salmon as they tried to fulfill their destiny. Some of the fish were so tired from struggling they just gave up. We pelted rocks at some of the seagulls in an attempt to run them off but there were just too many of them and in turn the seagulls injured and killed the salmon a greater pace. It was the cruelest display I had witnessed up here. I am supposed to feel that this is all just part of nature that this just the way it is. That may very well be but I had never been so involved in it all before,except when the cat I had as a child would bring home a half dead bird or mouse and play with it sadistically until it died. Here were these creatures trying their best to make it up stream for one last feeble attempt at having their fishy legacy live on, and it was to no avail. We could not help them, and even if we could save a few. It was their lot in life to eventually die while pursuing their goal. Such is the brutal nature of living for all of us.

We ended our excursion by saying good-bye to Braiden's' parents as they boarded the ferry for their own long journey home. After that Braiden had to work a few hours and I had the lunch shift at the restaurant, so I had just enough time to change and get there, with a quick kiss and a promise of having dinner with Zig and Terri. Off we went in our separate directions.

We had a nice dinner with Zig and Terri at the apartment, they cooked lasagna and surprise it involved no salmon or fish of any kind. After dessert, we decided to go out for a walk on our own, a very long walk to give Zig and Terri some alone time. We were going to spend the night at Steve's new apartment near the breakers. He eventually told us we could stay as long as we wanted if we helped him paint the place. It was a great offer so we jumped on it telling him we would only need accommodations until we found our own place.

I was wearing my new dress, it wasn't a really great dress because we had only a handful of shops here and more than half of those carried mostly souvenirs for tourists like those that come off cruise ships. Most of which are truly spectacular, like my favorite ocean liner the "Rotterdam" a ship that was so large it could not even come near the little dock to lay anchor. I was truly mesmerized by these ships. I often had trouble fathoming just how big these things were. So large they had to send little dinghies with the tourists in them.

Sometimes at Terri's' apartment I would sit out on the steps with my coffee in hand on some mornings just to watch the huge ships come to town, and dock, well as near as they could.

I would watch anytime I had the chance, contemplating life and just smiling peacefully to myself. There is something truly beautiful about ships and boats. Just the thought that they glided across the water gracefully and with purpose, I could appreciate this because they represented traits I did not feel I possessed.

We progressed over to Steve's place walking hand in hand a full moon overhead watching over us. It seemed like ages since Braiden and I had any moments resembling true romance. We found a bench near the water and sat for a short rest. The bench was old brown wood and splintering and smelling of creosote, you know the smell of which I speak, that smell usually off of telephone poles that resembles a mixture of crude oil and disinfectant on dry wood. I don't know why? It just does. In fact most all docks anywhere have this distinct stink as it were.

"Bray, can we talk?" my tone of voice did not seem like my own.

"So talk already." Braiden snapped.

"Oh come on now if your going to take that tone with me I will never speak to you again!" I huffed.

Braiden looked at me with a half grin, took my hands in his, and gave me his full attention "I am so sorry, please forgive me. I have just been stressed about work and finding us a place to live and weather or not we are even going to stay up here through the winter. I am sorry I haven't been around much lately either" then he just let out a deep sigh.

"We have been over all of this before. You're hardly ever around and when you are, you have been sleeping or you snap at me. I can't say I blame you, I know we need the money and it's been difficult just trying to live up here. Terri is wonderful but I know we are cramping her style"

All he said was " I agree, and I am going to take Tuesday off so we can go find a place of our own, I swear, until then just remember I love you and I have never said it before but I do, with all my heart, so bare with me."

Excuse me did I hear correctly that he said he loves me? Now after all these months and all the shit we have endured, he now loves me. I admit it caught me off guard and at any other time I would have been elated to here this, because I have waited so long for those words from him. But now I just felt more confused and slightly pissed off and thrown for a loop.

What can I say? I could have said I love you back, but I was not going to, at least not until I truly knew what I was doing, and where our tattered war torn relationship was headed. We moved off the bench at that point went over to the edge of the dock and sat with our feet dangling over the side. I liked to do this and it was fun, the large drop down to the water gave it some excitement, unless you actually fell in. We sat there for a while with our faces dimly lit by the mixture of moonlight and far off street lamps.

I did my best to gaze into his eyes "Bray, either we make it up here as a couple or we don't. But we have to let it run its course it will all be all right, you'll see. Trust me" did I in fact have that much faith? Was I lying? I sure sounded calm and self-assured. But I wasn't buying what my mouth was saying. Only time would tell if I was in deed a liar, or if everything would correct itself between us. I felt I really no longer needed him to give his love or approval of me. Have I become stronger? Am I changing into maturity? Will I grow wild teeth and perhaps a hump like some salmon? What the hell was happening to me!!!

It was almost midnight by the time we reached Steve's place. He was happy to see us and had our sleeping bags all laid out and ready for us. I told him I had to work the brunch shift and to get me up in the morning.

Before I went off to work Steve had made me coffee and eggs and toast. Wow! It was like a fancy hotel. Braiden, Steve and their new buddy Chris were going to paint the apartment today while I was away, and that night we were all going out to dinner and have a few drinks.

My workday was filled with all the usual pleasantries of

balancing trays like a performing seal and doing the bidding of pushy ungrateful patrons.

"Miss can I have another fork? I seemed to have dropped mine on the floor, and now it's all fuzzy." or "Excuse me waitress, our bill is wrong I ate the steak and it says here I had chicken, and my wife here never got her extra side of dressing but you charged us anyway." or my all time favorite. " Hey take this back it's not cooked all the way." To which sometimes you'd like to reply "Eat it anyway there is only a fifty-fifty chance you'll get sick from it. And there is only a slim margin that you'll croak from being sick. Stop whining!"

Okay, so waiting on people all day can make you cranky at times. You do have added benefits of sore feet and swollen ankles and wanting to collapse from exhaustion and you suddenly know how a plow horse feels. But you are getting tons of exercise and you have to remind yourself you are providing a portion of the world's hungry tummies with sustenance.

On my walk back home that evening I stopped in to Terri's' to collect the rest of my things.

"Hello? Terri are you here?" I announced myself loudly as I came into the room so as not to sneak up on her.

"Hey, how's it going?" she came at me with arms open for a big hug. She missed me and wanted to chat but I had to be off.

" I can't stay I am just here to get the rest of my stuff. I only want you to know how appreciative we are for all the kindness you have show for letting us live here. Bray, and I want to take you and Zig out for dinner on Thursday." I was talking and grabbing all the while.

"Yeah, that sounds good." She seemed pleased at this, and I left.

When I got back to Steve's I found they had finished painting and did a respectable job except for the blotchy areas around the windows and doors. Aside from the ceiling being pale yellow and the walls a dirty white, it looked decent.

I just tried to come up with something supportive, and

encouraging. "Wow, you guys did this all while I was gone? It looks, clean." They stood and grinned at me from ear to ear feeling they had accomplished a major task. Who am I to piss on their painting parade? After we all cleaned ourselves up and changed our clothes, it was time to head out to our first stop "The Narcoleptic Whale" It's a diner type place with home cooking, the usual fare, hamburgers, pot roast and grilled cheese and tonight they had a special of meatloaf. The sign said, "Just like your mother made."

I thought to myself "Gee, I hope not." We sat down and ordered and while we were waiting for our drinks and food, a man who had the appearance of someone shady on the corner wearing a long trench coat, who I expected to utter. " Hey,Psssst, wanna buy a duck?" approached us with a very furry pair of gray slippers.

"How you all doing this evening?" he asked without a drop of sincerity in his voice. We answered collectively "Fine" Then he continued and placed the slippers in my hands while he talked, they were the softest things I had ever held, I wondered what they were made out of?

" Good, I have got a deal for you. How would you like custom slippers out of get this, Baby Seal fur" I could actually feel the bile creep up my esophagus, and the look of terror move across my face. Braiden on the other hand, had a looked at the man as if he had just told him he shot his dog, not once but twice.

Then he spoke "Sir, and I use that term in the broadest sense of the word, I'd sooner wear earmuffs made out of Bambi's mother". The guy then mumbled some rather unfriendly words and left us to eat our meal. I am aware that some people make their livings in very different ways. You take what your surroundings have to give you, and use it to your advantage. I do have difficulty agreeing with some of these ways. But I do understand different cultures have different views and who am I to judge.

It was difficult to eat after that but we somehow managed. We finished our burgers and sodas, quickly I may add. It was then time to stroll on over to that fine upscale strip establishment. "The Funky Penguin."

It was a little sleazy hole in the wall and the only nude bar in town, but it was sort of fun, and I was the only woman there not getting paid to be in attendance, so I got special treatment. The place was the size of a large elevator, smoky and filled with men. A tune by the band Soft Cell "Tainted love" blared out from the sound system, while a very unattractive woman danced with the pole naked, on a stage the size of a five dollar bill.

I followed Braiden and Chris and Steve to the only available table left by the back door. The young lady (I chuckle even using that term) finished her dance got off the stage and sauntered past us to the room where all the strippers changed and hung out, a dressing room of sorts. Then the next one up was better looking there was talk around the bar that they imported her form Seattle? Or Vancouver?

She had long dark hair, pouty lips. (I have never been totally clear on what the hell pouty lips were but apparently she had them and they are attractive to men) she started to dance and remove her top, then she took off her scarf and started to use it in rather lude way (well I will let your imagination fill in the rest). Just as she was about to remove her skirt the dressing room door flew open as if the hinges were being torn out. It was the first dancer, and she passed us with a fury reserved only for charging bulls and mad strippers.

"You Bitch!" she yelled as she approached the stage, fists clenched. She now stood at the stage and the dancer kept dancing trying to finish her act. "You Bitch, that's my scarf, do you hear me, who said you could use it you..........!" her words slurred from too much free booze I could tell this was going to be good.

At this point the rather unattractive one took the other one by her hair and pulled her off the stage. She literally dragged her off the stage. Everyone watched anxiously at the ensuing cat fight.

First a slap, then a kick, then they exchanged scratches.

As one of the bouncers tried to step in to break it up, he was intercepted.

"Don't break them up Phil, let them fight" one of the patrons shouted. Then Phil shoved this man aside, and then was hit by a chair from nowhere. After that shit was flying everywhere. Bottles were breaking chairs were becoming airborne and we decided it was time to go. By this time the strippers were throwing blows at each other, fists swinging, it was getting ugly. Then the guy that was hit by the other guy smashed a bottle over his attackers head. At that point the other patrons started to fight amongst themselves and then the other three strippers came out to get involved. It looked like a staged bar room brawl in an old western movie.

Chris and Steve ran out the front door and when Braiden and I saw a table fly by us decided it was time to make a break for it out the back door. I knew the police would be advancing here real quick. I was moving slowly as the fascination was too much for me. Braiden grabbed me by the arm and flung me out the back door just inches from the bouncer who figured Braiden was a threat to me.

"Come on your moving to slow". Then Bray noticed the bouncer or rather I should say "Talking Wall."This guy was bald and weighed 300 lbs and stood easily six foot six. You could not be sure if he was wearing a vest or if his arms were so big that his sleeves just fell off from fear.

He asked me "Is this guy bothering you little lady?"

"You know Bray, all I have to do is say yes and this guy will kill you" I whispered gleefully.

Braiden turned rather pale and said to me "Please tell this guy its all okay" so I obliged.

"You owe me big time for this one" I turned back to Mr. Bouncer man and replied "Its Okay this is my husband he didn't mean to get rough, we will make up soon I promise" I smiled sweetly and he let us continue high tailing it out of there as he went into the bar to check on all the commotion.

We had made it around the front just when the police arrived and were hauling people away. Good Times! It was a brisk walk back to Steve's place that evening. Yes, the weather was cool but mostly it was because we wanted to be safely away from the derelict drunks the bored cops and the belligerent strippers.

The next morning I found myself drawn once again to the sunken vessel located by Steve's place at the end of the pier. I would often peer down at over the rail, and stare at this submerged boat that lay below. I liked to contemplate things, just things, as it laid there.

It was our last night at Steve's as we had just rented a place and we could move in the next day, a place of our own. Home was now for the time being a studio apartment. It was cute, had a large bay window and room for a sofa bed. I suppose for eight hundred and fifty bucks a month that this was a bargain. I was not happy with the cost, but luckily we had paid our rent up through the end of September and that would give us time to decide how much longer we wanted to be up here. We had something new to consider, having recently been informed by Terri of a new incentive check that we could be eligible for. This dividend thing would be paid to us if we could manage to live up here for a year. It had something to do with the pipeline. You'd be in the position to receive close to a grand, I think?

As I gazed down into the wet depths below, Braiden came up behind me and said "Doris you got to come with me, I met this couple who own this boat and they have been sailing all around the world in it. They want us to come and have a piece of homemade pie with them." my brain was wrapping around this idea and you know if this was any other place I would be skeptical that this couple would hogtie us and wear our intestines for a hat. But hay this being Ketchikan and all, I said

"Why not!"

The couple seemed sane enough, their boat or should I say yacht was spacious and clean and attractive and I could fantasize about the life they lead. He was a retired business- man and this was his trophy of a second wife I would imagine. Her name was Kathy and his was John. The pie was pretty good. We bid them farewell and we were on our way. All in all it was almost an uncomfortable experience in its pleasantness.

Even though we had many friendly times up here my enthusiasm of continuing to live up here was waning a little more, day by day. Sure I had a good job, now a place to stay and Braiden as far as I could tell was behaving and being more attentive. I just had a feeling that there was something Braiden was hiding and I also really did not want to live out the rest of my life as a waitress in Alaska. It would have been easy for me to fall into a trap like that. Deep down it wasn't my ideal life, it could be a good life, but not my ideal life, even though I am still not sure what my ideal life actually is? I was definitely going to have to give it more thought.

To shake things up even more Braiden received news that Val's ex boyfriend Eddie had been shot to death. It seems that he was, caught in "the act" by a jealous husband. "Oh, well, it figures." was all I could muster. Its not that I have become cold hearted, I just felt that hey if you play with the proverbial fire you're gonna get your ass planted in the ground like a roasted pig at some point. Cheating on a spouse or lover is generally no laughing matter. You're going to hurt someone with your actions. Therefore it is best to remain loyal.

Now, there are a few women that I have known that if I were romantically involved with them, well, I would cheat on them to. Let's face it some women are nagging, overbearing, emasculating shrews. Don't get me wrong, there are also men out there in the world like that who are emotionally unavailable, unsupportive and uncaring of their partners needs. Accept the consequences that arise if you're going to end up in bed with a person that is already involved with another person.

I had an epiphany as of late, about that word, consequence. It means taking responsibility for your actions.Iit means thinking ahead at what that outcome may be, the possibility that things may turn out in your favor if your intentions are good. But, if somehow you're skimming over the other side of the coin, thinking it doesn't apply to you and pay no heed to ill feelings. Well then, shit can happen.

My smugness often startles my own mind. I am no saint. For the record, I don't feel saints exist. All of us have within, the capability to carry out a positive or negative actions. It's how we live on a daily basis that factor in things like, how we respond to other people's actions toward us. Or what they have done to us, how we perceive the world as it is, and how we want it to be. The conclusions are drawn by the brain and therefore acted upon as it sees fit. This all sounds cliché but that's what life turns into some times one friggin huge cliché.

Moving into our new digs was a fairly simple thing to do. We didn't even have to buy any furniture, because a sofa bed had been given to us by a Saxon tribe member. He unfortunately didn't have money to pay his cab fare. Braiden made a deal with him and it worked out great for us. Not so great for him I imagine, as he probably had to explain to his wife as to where the couch ended up. Now if we could just locate a table? We did have a small closet that could accommodate our clothing because we had very little of it,just mainly what we came up here with and only a few new pieces. I got along just fine with boots and jeans on most of my days off.

CHAPTER FIFTEEN

"Take the long way home"

I had recently got a new haircut, a drastic new haircut. It was short and severe but really easy to take care of. I felt the need of having brown hair with blonde highlights was way past its cute phase. Besides, you didn't really see too many shag haircuts any more, well

not up here anyways. I had made the difficult decision to let it also return to its natural un-enhanced color of mousy brown. It was time for me to have a less immature and weak style, as I want to believe I have become more grounded in my personality.

I also got used to wearing less makeup. Because make up was not that prevalent here and I liked the clean look. It somehow suited me, and my new hair. I was morphing into a different person, what kind exactly remained to be seen. Come to think of it I felt I was a lot more relaxed and calm just in general. I had grown up in the short, frantic, grueling time I was here, compared to how I used to feel about myself and life and how I fit into the whole scheme of things.

Thursday had arrived and on this fine afternoon Terri and I were spending it together. Later we were meeting the guys for dinner because Zig was heading out again on his buddies fishing boat. Braiden and I were footing the dinner bill, as our way of thanking them like we wanted to. Terri and I headed out on her skiff, which, in this particular case, is a small green colored boat like craft about twelve feet long,with no cover and only a v-shaped windshield to block the bugs and the water spray. It was also well equipped with a good strong motor and easy steering.

We decided to drive it all around Pennock today. We had a couple of beers and headed around the far right side of the island when Terri told me to take the wheel as she took a break. What she really wanted me to do was master the fine art of maneuvering a water going vessel. The feeling of power was fabulous. I was driving and amazed at how simple it was. As I guided the skiff it hit me, so, this is what true freedom is like, the wind in your hair and a quiet ocean spread out in front of you, the spray coming off the water, the loud incessant humming of the motor as you bounce off the waves underneath. Making that slapping sound as you hit. It's lovely! Albeit, in a jack hammering sort of way.

Pennock Island has trees everywhere, lush and with deep colors that you'd expect on an island with few inhabitants. It's just a mass of beautiful trees and some rocky beach, the kind of rocks that resembled, well, rocks. I had only observed five real cabins on the island. We pulled the boat off to the shore and parked it so we could drink beers and talk about life. This was great!

"So, how are you and Zig really getting along?" I felt we were far enough out of earshot to speak freely.

"Well, okay I guess, I like having time all to myself but lets face it you can't very well have a meaningful love life with someone who wants to be gone so much."

I had to agree. "Yeah, I know. I feel the same way. Bray, has acted strange it seems, since shortly after the time we got up here. I haven't decided if he is bored with me or tired of working. He says' it has been stressful for him. I believe it; I just don't know where I fit into his life?"

Terri nodded, and we both took a swig of refreshing brewed beverage. After a while we figured it was time o head back home to get cleaned up and dressed. We approached the mainland it seemed to me we reached it much too soon. I felt a large tug at my heart I was a little sad because I realized I loved Ketchikan but could not live here. But I loved being here. So I was conflicted. I was told a few weeks ago by a close friend that you either love it here or hate it, that spending an entire winter up here will either strengthen a relationship or destroy it forever. I then stepped off the skiff and let out the biggest belch I had ever experienced. So loud that two guys passing by applauded. I shrugged my shoulders and said "Must be the waves?"

Dinner at the "The Velvet Moose" was grand. An elegant place that we never went to. Red velvet curtains, solid heavy wood tables and chairs and lighting that must have been about eighty years old, with stained glass and crystals. A magnificent dining establishment, that harkened back to those gold rush days. Okay so I am laying it on a little thick, it was very elegant except for the mounted moose head on the wall and the eight-foot tall stuffed moose in the corner wearing a tuxedo. It's a pricey but this was a special occasion as it would also be Zig's' last fishing trip for the season.

"Let the wine flow, I'm buying" Braiden said in a rather uptight but happy tone. "I bet you're glad this is the last trip for the season. What are you going to do for the winter?

"In fact what does anyone do for the winter up here? We have never really discussed that?" I asked hesitantly as I really did not want to know what harshness befalls the year round inhabitants of this secluded world.

Terri answered me "Zig usually sleeps through much of the winter like a hibernating bear. The rest of the time he helps me out and then of course he goes to visit his mom and dad. Other people spend their off time in more interesting way, like making sculptures out of fish bones and moose tipping." Ah! Then a good laugh was shared by all.

It was then dropped on me that Braiden was going with him on this trip. Shit! But I would be okay? Would I ? Sure.

Braiden had been gone two and a half days and would be returning this evening. I had enjoyed the "me time". I took the day off from work, so I could have a long leisurely stroll down to the pier by Steve's before I got ready for tonight. I had not been there in a while and I enjoyed the pier because others rarely ventured out there.

Tourist season was winding down and coming to an end, they were fewer and farther between. I packed myself a nice lunch and went to my favorite spot. It was peaceful and nice and I sat on the bench and took out my sandwich. Baloney and Swiss, my favorite. I took a few bites and then a very large black bird, a common raven I think, standing about a foot and a half tall weighing in at I would estimate about two or three pounds, sat next to me. I gave him a piece and took another bite. Another bird landed, okay? Another crust, then five more landed and started to surround me. In my throat I gulped and ever so slowly gathered my backpack and left my sandwich and ran to the end of the pier to escape the swarm that Hitchcock himself could not have choreographed better.

I hung out here until the feeding frenzy subsided. I leaned over to study the sunken boat that always brings a much appreciated calmness to me. This puts things in perspective for me. This boat was twenty-five feet down and resting on the bottom. I believe it had been there for many years with that old worn look. It has no paint, no markings; mainly just the front end of it peered up at me. It looked like it belonged in a pirate movie. The mast still attached to it with parts of shredded sail. It was fascinating. I stared at it for a long while trying to make up a story as to what had happened.

There was a great battle over a fishing expedition and the owner threw the captain over board. Before the captain hit the water he blew a hole in the side of it with his gun to sink it.

He let out a sinister laugh, and threw his head back. "Take that you scurve of the sea, arrrrr, I shall teach you to cheat me out of my wages and drink my rum."

Okay, so maybe that's not what happened. Maybe it just sunk in a storm and the owner felt it was too much hassle to retrieve it. I stood there absorbed in my own world and a shadow passed about a few feet over my head. It was an eerie shadow and triangular in shape and large. I would have guessed it to be a kite if this was any other part of the world. Then I felt the ominous presence land next to me about three feet away.

I was afraid to look and for the first minute I had every intention of not moving at all. But my curiosity got the better of me and at first I peeked out of the corner of my eye, not turning my head. I could only see a large moving shape. Okay I will turn my head slowly, so excruciatingly slow that it hurt. My eyes followed my head Pennock was now directly in front of me. Then open waterway, then finally my gaze landed on it. I am sure my mouth dropped open, I didn't even breathe. Only seeing this most humbling of all majestic sights.

It was an American Bald Eagle and it was real and it was close and I was scared because it was about three feet tall and it probably could carry me off if it felt like it but damn it was gorgeous and no one was around to see it with me and no one would believe this. My heart skipped and it looked at me like I was an insignificant spec on his earth. He was magnificent, spectacular, and I was falling in love. Slowly he opened his wings and it was a good six feet of wingspan. Off he went creating a breeze as he flew away. I decided to walk back home as nothing could top this the day had peaked for me. Truly the Eagle had landed! The curtain had come down nothing could top this wondrous sight. It was time to head for home.

In a small town its been said that everybody knows your business before you do. I had come to have many friends in my short time here some I would even try to stay connected with when and if I left. I decided to take my daily stroll to the post office before I went back home to the apartment. When my eyes beheld an unusual sight of which I could not have imagined or did I understand. Braiden was coming out of Kim's apartment?

Fastening his belt and glancing around, then ran his customary hand through his lustrous mane. I was stunned and stared and just stood there waiting for that cartoon weight of ten thousand pounds to hit my head. He was at sea? He was out on a fishing boat? How long had this been going on? What the fuck! They did not see me as I peered around the corner, and I really did not feel this was the time or place to confront him with this new development. I needed space and time to think about it all and let it soak in, as I did not want to create a scene. Also I was afraid I would kick his sorry butt from here to Canada right now. What else could I do? I sat on the pier and cried.

He was due home at our place tonight. I did not want to be there so I asked Terri if I could stay with her. I told her all about my predicament and she was shocked but Zig knew something was going on and said it was not his place to monitor his brother even though he did nod condone what he was doing. He also said that in fact Braiden was on the boat for a day and a half. How exactly that information was supposed to make me feel better was beyond me.

That night Braiden went home to an empty apartment. But Terri did get a phone call.

"Hello? Oh hi. Yeah she's sleeping here tonight…I think you had better discuss that with her…no I am not putting her on the phone, I will have her call you…okay, ya bye." It was nice to have a friend that would watch out for your feelings.

"Thanks Terri, I will get a hold of him tomorrow, possibly in the groin area." I never failed to amuse myself. "No I will talk to him after I figure out what the heck to do now."

Terri always the dear person said. "You're welcome to stay here for as long as you want. We can work something out." It did make me feel a little better.

"Thanks that's good to know. I think right now I am just going to hit the hay. Good night." The bed was cold, the night air coming through the window was cold, my heart was cold, and my brain was tired of thinking for tonight.

It was business as usual the next day. Braiden was back on his cab job and I went to put in my shift working with Kim as if nothing had been discovered. It was the most difficult thing I have ever had to do. "Kim how could you?" was all I kept asking myself. I wanted to confront her, to throw salad in her face with dressing on it. Or at the very least, take her to Kodiak Island to be eaten by bears. Instead I handled it like a grown up and sat down at the bar to have a drink after my shift ended.

"Hey, Joe give me a Tom Collins."

"Sure Doris, rough shift?" Joe spoke as he handed over my drink.

"You don't know the half of it. Thanks." I hopped off the barstool and decided to sit at the table by the window and stare out blankly. It seemed like the right thing to do.

"Hi Doris, wow that was a rough shift wasn't it?" well what do you know its my arch nemesis Kim. She sat down without me motioning her to. I guess she is still under the misconception that you can have intercourse with your friend's man and we would be civilized. I said nothing, but kept to my drink.

Her clueless perky demeanor was more than I could stand. "Joe, another one please." I pointed to my glass.

"So, Kim what's new? Anything shaking besides your ass?" I hissed.

"What is that supposed to mean?" she chuckled

"You're funny." I received my drink and just was not willing to let this one slide. "You slut, how the hell long have you been screwing my boyfriend? I thought we were friends? You Bitch." her eyes widened and I slammed my drink down and proceeded with a nice upper cut to her jaw.

The table turned over the glass hit the floor and she lay there crying and proceeded to explain. "It was all his idea, you have to believe me? Please Doris, "sob" please this isn't fair. Braiden is slime." She said scurrying to get her footing.

"Yeah, well he's my slime." She was standing now and although she has a good five inches over me is no match for a vicious rodent such as myself. I picked up the wood chair and swung at her and she proceeded to grab a serving tray. This was it; of course it was bound to happen. My life had finally become a classic western movie. At this point a crowd was gathering and our boss was yelling.

"Ladies please! Stop! Stop right now!" But it was too late, I was too far into the moment and threw the chair, it went through the front window with a crash, and then I lunged for that long blonde hair. Pulling as we both rolled around on the floor. I punched her in the nose just like I was fending off a shark attack, I heard a crunch, and the blood gushed. I had broken it that was when I knew I had had won.

She backed off and people rushed to her rescue and everyone was urged back to their jobs. "Doris I am sorry to do this but in light of what just happened you're fired. I won't press any charges if Kim won't. But you have to turn in your stuff and leave now. I will have someone deliver your paycheck. Minus what the cost is to fix the damage."

He was a good boss, it was a good job but it was over. But, damn I felt good! I said a few quick good byes. I swear a few of the guys were a little turned on by this whole scene and one handed me his phone number.

I took my time walking to the pay phone, and called Braiden at the "Crab Cab" only stating it was urgent and I needed to see him at the "Pasta Tree" as soon as he got off work. Nothing left to do now but sit and wait. And eat, and wait, and think some more.

We had a long and drawn out discussion. It went nowhere, it just consisted of a lot of blaming and finger pointing and perhaps a cold shake dumped in his lap.

The next few days for me were a blur of sad moments and quiet streets. No longer did I have to contemplate whether I would remain in Ketchikan or not. The choice had been made for me and without my input.aside from me instigating that little incident that resulted in my job termination, and told I could not set foot in there again. But, hey, my time here was now winding down, and I knew what path was laid out before me.

Dear "Sparky,"

Long time no contact. Hope this letter finds you well and in good spirits? Sorry I haven't written before now. Been real busy, you know how that goes. In case you had not heard, I did go to Alaska after all, arriving here shortly after last seeing you. The weather here and the people here have been more pleasant than I thought. I have eaten many fish and fastened a hut out of leaves and scraps of wood I found.

I had a steady waitress job up until a few days ago. Really! And I have learned to drive a boat and oh yeah, I cut my hair. I am now however having a hard time admitting it, but, you may have been correct in your insights regarding Braiden, and some of my choices in life. Things have not turned out as planned up here. I am not sure what I was expecting? I suppose I was trying to run away from parts of myself. I proved it isn't possible, can't be done. We often take our troubles with us wherever we go. No matter how fast or how far we run from them. I find myself in an unpleasant situation now and even though I am not really confused about it, I have apprehensions. I may have to come back to California. Trouble is I don't know how to go about it? What to do now? How do I leave?

Until our paths cross again.

Big hugs

Your buddy, "D"

I imagine Sparky at his kitchen table, drinking his coffee and reading the letter. I wasn't expecting a letter back so soon. Sparky must have sent one out immediately after mine arrived.

Dear "D"

I was glad to get a letter from you. Unlike Ketchikan, the weather here is still like the people, irritating and uncomfortable. Nice to here you finally learned a trade. I am sure building huts will come in handy later in life. Sorry to hear you lost your job. But now that you have some experience you'll get other employment. As for being right, well I was hoping to be wrong in my assumption of Braiden, what ever he did. I would have rather I'd been wrong for your sake.

I have enrolled in a few college filmmaking courses and looks like I will be staying around here a while. I also got a job and I am in the process of finding my own apartment. I will get a two bedroom one and in case you ever need it you are welcome to stay. I am sure however things turn out, and what ever conclusion you come to, I know it will be solely your decision, because you have never taken anyone else's advice or suggestions. You are a head strong and stubborn person. And I believe that you have always been tougher, both mentally and physically than you give yourself credit for. Call me when you get home and I'll take you for a burger.

Until then

Keep your spirits and your pants up!

Your buddy "S"

I sat on what had become my favorite creosote smelling bench folding the letter and returning it to the envelope. I had to smile to myself because it seemed like the right thing to do. What remained now for me to do was purchase airfare out of here, notify my father and then start with my many difficult good-byes.

I was not ready to leave the bench. I really wasn't ready to leave Ketchikan. I continued to gaze out over the water, noticing that today was calm, dark and beautiful. I no longer saw it as a threat. It was now darkness covering what could now hold new possibilities of unknown that lay beneath, of promise and of anticipation for what was to come into my life.

Not for what was on the way out. A far cry from how I first saw it. A couple passed by, walking hand in hand. A new boat was pulling into the dock. The air smelled fresh, clean and new, up here it always smells like the air after a rainfall. A group of clouds was forming up overhead. Seagulls flying and making those seagull sounds that reminded me of that time on the beach, when I wished I was as free as them. Car horns honking, I bet some of the drivers on their way to jobs. I used to have a job. I will probably have one again someday.

Returning back to California might be a shock to my system after this sort of life. I would be returning to the fresh water to spawn, not literally. In a way it would be my version of carrying on my legacy. Start college like Sparky? Start a career? See what harsh reality had to throw at me. But unlike months before, harsh reality could not bring me down ever again after what I have learned. Going back would mean staying with mom and dad once again, if they let me? If not then I would go stay with Sparky. Or get a place of my own. I had choices I had ideas. I could do this. The difficult part was going to be ending it with Braiden.

I sighed and a few people walked by. Another boat came into dock and of course the scene would not have been complete without the large black raven that landed to sit with me on the creosote bench. It cawed and looked around.

"I imagine you have come to bid me adieu?" He looked at me and I looked at him and he cawed once again. "Yeah, I figured you might." My companion and I lingered for a few minutes longer.

CHAPTER SIXTEEN

"Over the hills and far away"

"What can I say? What can I do so you'll forgive me?" Braiden was begging at this point and I tell you for a really attractive man it was most unattractive.

"Look this just isn't going to work any longer. You cheated on me. I know it now. I was debating with myself back and forth, thinking you meant it when you said loved me. So, you could not be capable of intimacy with someone else. And yes even though I am sure you have done it before, this time I found out about it. Let alone with someone who I called a friend. The really sad thing is I was starting to like it up here. I almost felt we could make it, and make it though the winter. I had a job I felt good about. I made close friendships I learned to enjoy a rougher lifestyle. Then you had to go and screw it all up for me. I don't know if I can forgive you or if I even want to?"

"I told you nothing happened; we shared some weed, a couple of joints that's all. Had a few laughs…okay maybe kissed a little? That's all." Nothing was alleviating my doubts. In a way him talking, just made things worse.

"Come on lets not go over this again. You need to be honest with yourself, if not me. I saw you fixing your belt, what else could that mean other than at some point your pants were undone. It explains so much. Why you're so tired, why we have been less than intimate and why you have been sneaking around. On top of the way you have acted towards me, towards us while we have been up here. I find it difficult to believe you. Face it, you're quite a good-looking guy, and women are attracted to you. And after all you are only a male with natural urges and if given the opportunity, I know you go for it every chance you get. I suppose I have been delusional thinking I could be enough for you."

We had been at this all morning, just a continuation from last night, and it was getting tiresome. "Look the reason I have been tired all the time and our sex life has suffered is I have been afraid of being too committed to you. I don't want to settle down. I am not ready, and you're too young. It scares me that I love you too much."

Oh, please can you believe this load of shit. Still you can't blame the guy for trying. "Love me too much? I don't fucking believe it. What else you got? Surly you can come up with something better than that?" I sat on the couch with arms folded.

"Okay, I didn't want to tell you this but I have been dealing drugs, yea, it's true. And that big yacht you and I kayaked out to was my dealer boss. It's the truth I swear, but I have stopped now and he is trying to kill me so I was hiding out at Kim's until it all blew over."

Wow, Nope not buying it. Arms still folded. "I cannot believe you would come up with a story that far fetched. But I think it was a good effort and you almost have convinced yourself." I stared in his deep brown eyes and almost saw a glimmer of remorse. Oh, no I cannot fall for him again. I will not do it.

"I have to get ready for my going away party at Terri's now. I will be away for a few hours. Do whatever you want, and you can sleep on the sofa bed tonight. I will sleep in the sleeping bag on the floor when I get in." I knew he would probably go drinking, or over to that floozy Kim's place. I didn't much give a flying sack of testicles what he did at this point. I had to get dressed.

Going away party, ready or not here I come. All my buddies were in attendance; Harry even came to offer me a marriage proposal if I would change my mind and stay.

"No Harry I don't think you could handle me" I said and we chuckled. Zig was also there to give support, and Val, and her new boyfriend Joe the bartender from my old job.

"Hi Joe, surprised to see you here? I hear you're going out with Val? Is my face still on the wanted poster at the restaurant?"

He chuckled and said in return. "Well, if it isn't the outlaw! Oh, I'm scared! And there is a ten thousand dollar bounty on your head. I don't know whether to hug you or turn you in.!" he smiled and we hugged. Good choice I thought as he is rather cute. I turned around and Zig was standing before me.

"Zig, with all that has happened could I trust you to keep a watchful eye over your little brother. I still love him and I am still not really sure what is going on in that pretty little head of his."

Zig cocked his head a bit to one side. "Yes, of course, I always look out for him." At this point I pulled out a letter I had written a few days ago.

"And, later when I am far enough away can you give him this." I handed him the envelope and he put it into his pocket.

"Doris my friend I will miss you." said a sweet and familiar voice behind me. And the moment was reminiscent of "This is your life." I somehow expected to see Hugh Downs. But no it was Terri.

"Hey, I am going to miss you most of all." I then threw my arms around her and started to cry a bit as Val came up to join in.

"We had some good times! We have been through a lot in these few short months. Please say that you won't forget me and that you'll keep in touch?" We all nodded, let go of each other and grabbed the closest beer we could find, to ease the parting of our ways.

The hours passed, the drinks flowed and I was basking in all the attention, from this decent sized crowd. The only ones who were not there were Kim and Braiden. Big fucking deal! The gathering in my opinion was a success.

Saying good-bye to Braiden was going to be difficult but saying farewell to all my buddies who I had grow to love was even more of a difficult experience than I had anticipated. The party had to eventually come to an end, and I left Terri's place, to head back to our apartment. I knew it was going to be my last walk from her place to mine.

No more girl chats or grabbing a drink after a rough day. No more making dinner with her and Val and hanging out like we were sisters. I may never feel that close to any women again in my life. After all, I had never felt it before in my life with my own sister. I crawled into the sleeping bag Braiden slept on the couch where he may very well have been ever since I left for the party. On the floor were at least half dozen empty beer bottles. My sleep was almost non existent, and very unsatisfactory. I watched him sleep though, but he was more passed out than asleep.

After I woke I ate a simple breakfast consisting of a bagel with cream cheese and a cup of coffee. I finished packing the last of my belongings while Braiden had gone to gas up the cab. The only thing I had not yet done was phone my parents and let them know I was returning. I sort of dreaded the fact that I was returning at all. I had put it off as long as possible.

Going back meant I was going back to them, for however long that would be. And the gloating at what they perceived as yet another poor judgment call by me. Rubbing my nose in it like some untrained dog. Letting the family know of my impending and less than victorious return to the Bay Area, was a necessary evil and something I had to do.

Why? Well, because I needed to be picked up from the Oakland airport. As I dialed the phone number I took a deep breath and prepared for them picking up the other end "click" here we go.

"Hi, Mom its Doris, and I am coming home today and need a ride from the airport." Dead silence then I heard a sort of scream and then weeping and mumbling and finally my father was handed the phone.

"Hi, Doris? Your mother is flailing about and sobbing, do you have any idea why?" he asked cautiously not knowing why mother was acting in this fashion.

"Hi Dad, good to hear your voice. Yes I do. Listen I just told mom that I was coming home today flight on #187 on Alaska Airlines and I need someone to pick me up at the Oakland airport terminal at five o'clock. Do you think you can do it?"

Dad understood it all now "Oh, now that makes sense, sure I can get you a ride, your brother is in from Chicago for a visit, and I am sure he will pick you up. Five o'clock, Alaska Airlines at Oakland Airport, I got it. No problem. I love you and good bye." As I said thank you and I loved him, I also heard him say to mom "Jesus! Helen, can you control yourself? "Bye dad, love you". I hung up the receiver. Well, now that's taken care of the stage was set, my destination was now set in stone and I exhaled. It was now the beginning of my departure.

Braiden had asked, or rather begged, if he could give me a ride to the ferry. He said it was the least he could do. He was correct in that thought, I agreed. He placed my small carry on bag in the trunk along with my trusty backpack and we headed out. In the short cab ride I was silent and found myself reflecting on our surreal adventures together up to this moment.

He tried a few times to engage me in light conversation. But I preferred staring out the window at the last view I would get of this odd city. Some of its older buildings that I swear resemble a movie studio back lot. The faces of it's residents, some standing and talking on the corner, others walking down the street or heading into one of the many bars. It was an average day here.

Ketchikan is a mellow sort of place, and I realized part of the reason I smoked less pot up here was because it was a mellow place, and in need of no assistance to make it so. The sky was the usual gray, with a tinge of fall moving in. A few people I knew saw me in the cab and waved and smiled. Maybe in one hundred years this place would appear again much like "Brigadoon" with Fred Astair.

Maybe in less than a hundred years I could find myself here again? After the embarrassment I had suffered at my own hands in my own bar brawl wore off. People do forget, don't they? And of course, it depends on if Braiden and I ever manage to get back on friendly terms.

Even though it has only been about eight months since I was last in California I could somehow barely recall what it was like there? Or rather, what I was like there? The first time meeting Braiden on the front steps of the quaint old house in Alameda. How I adored him and hung on his every word. Hoping someday I could be as smart and spiritually in touch with life as he was.

The first time we made love and how awkward it all was. I had only two sexual encounters before that and they were less than stunning, but with Bray, it was awkward. Fulfilling, but awkward, as it actually took place in a coat closet at a party we went to. We got much better at it from practice in the months following. I thought of that fateful Halloween party and how it seems like it was part of some other person's life. Oscar, my poor dearly departed Oscar. I will not easily forget you. Maybe I will take up some form of gardening to remind me of that sweet, steamy and heart wrenching encounter with you.

Then I thought of my parents protesting my individuality and my rebellion.How would they accept me now as I am? Have they ever accepted me? Could I attempt to correct my past indiscretions or should I even acknowledge them? In fact I may just put them all behind me and forge ahead. I would miss most all of the relationships I made here, the friendships and bonds of real and honest people. Terri and Val most of all, they taught me I could love a man, and be my own person. Maybe I just had to find the right man, I knew Braiden probably loved me in his own special way but he wasn't the right one for me, or was he?

Maybe I am making some awful mistake? I could turn back now. Tell him to stop the cab. Hide up here forever and forgive him. Ah yes, forgive him. How can I do that now? Well I could forgive him, it is up to me. But I am willing to do that? If I absolved him now, too soon he may just pull some other shit on me, thinking it was somehow okay to do. So, no, I am not ready yet. I needed time and lots of distance between us to see how I really felt.

I will miss this place, this odd and wonderful part of the earth. I have grown reluctantly fond of it. How can just being in a different place teach a person so much? I learned valuable survival, kayaking and work skills. Hard work skills, damn hard work skills that I could not have picked up anywhere else. Things I don't ever want to do again. I may not eat salmon for a few years, or ever again in my life for that matter either.

I won't soon forget the magnificent night sky filled with more stars in the heavens than you have believed were present. Or the sharp clean cold of the air as you breath it in on a early morning, or the natural loveliness of all the sea creatures, in their own environment, not stuffed behind glass partitions in an aquarium or unable to interact with each other. The sight is far more charming than any animated cartoon. They are free and sort of frolic, if in fact things were ever to frolic, it would be them.

I must say all in all Alaska and my experience of it was not one of a hostile environment, well at least not where I was. I have to admit I was more hostile to it than it was to me. I have never really been sure if I was fighting myself, my troubled relationship with Bray? Or was I fighting the "ever looming" onset, of becoming a responsible adult? Perhaps, a fine blend of all of those, coming to the realization that sometimes, the wilderness is within ourselves. I infected this place with my negative judgmental views. I was a bad influence on the gentle balance that already exists here.

I never did get to see Aurora Borealis as everyone has talked about it. I tend to feel it was some sort of a legend like Jack'a'lope or Bigfoot. Many have told of its remarkable beauty, and I heard by a few people up here that supposedly saw it first hand at some point in their lives. Maybe if I had stayed up here longer I might have had the opportunity.

I now believe it is possible to see more beauty in many forms. Not like having the strict guidelines of it upon my arrival here months ago. Arriving here as a snotty bratty punk with long polished nails and an attitude that these people were backwards, their lifestyle was substandard and I was some how above them, I held the belief that I was one wild tough little shit. How silly I was. How naive and unenlightened.

This place does nothing but breed, tough, sturdy and down to earth residents. The few Eskimos and Saxon Indians that I had the pleasure of encountering held an aura about them of strength, dignity and pride. The surroundings I believe are partially to praise for this. They seemed to have always been aware of the greatness of this state and the magic that it holds.

Ketchikan and all of Alaska need to be held in higher regard than it is. I see that now. This place cannot be duplicated, cannot be replaced and is delicate and can easily be destroyed. It is more majestic than any man made structure, more precious than Shangri La and more awe inspiring than the Sistine chapel, in all it's forceful beauty. I leave humbled by it. I now head back to California stronger, more self-assured and self-aware.

Realizing that I had gone from a shallow indulgent bit of fluff to someone I could almost now be proud of. Was I done growing? Was this the best I could be? I must say my journey has probably just started on the way to being a fully formed human. I have a long way to go but now the task doesn't seem quite as daunting or imposing. Being thrown back into California will most likely give me some culture shock. Both states hold beauty of there own, but Californians tend to focus more on the pursuit of gold as opposed to honor the mountains from where the gold came from.

We had now arrived at the dock. Braiden parked the car and grabbed my belongings out of the trunk.

"I'm not sure what to tip you?" I said nervously trying to be funny.

"Tell me you don't want to leave, tell me you'll forgive me and stay."

What could I say? How could I answer? "If I am not on that ferry one of us will regret it, maybe not today maybe not tomorrow but soon and for the rest of our lives."

Where the hell did that come from? Wait, was that from Casablanca? He put the bags down and kissed me like he did when we had first started going out together. It was a hard passionate seductive kiss. And I was faltering. Big time. This was a mistake, leaving is a mistake and staying would be a mistake. Shit! Was I ever one severely confused life form? How am I ever going to get on that blasted ferry and get out of here?

"I love you, I mean it. Please don't go. I will make everything better than it has been. I swear." I know it's too simple bit the scent of his body was enough to reconsider my actions. He held me close, and I felt sad. I had not really let myself feel that before but I felt as if I was being ripped away from part of my own heart. I held him only a few moments longer or I would surely not be able to ever leave. I released him, his touch, his scent, and his body.

"I have to go or I will miss the ferry and my flight." I grabbed my backpack and small carry on and off I went.

"I'll pay you for your ticket, I'll reimburse you. Stay! How about just a little while longer? We can take it slow." He yelled as I stepped on the transport and gave my pass to the ferry master. The time had now come for me to depart and take my short trip to Gravina Island, for my flight to my stop in Seattle as I head for home.

Could I consider it home any longer? I may be searching for a place that truly felt like home, my home, for some time to come. Until then I would have to settle in once again in the same house with the dreaded parental units, to figure out my next move.

As I stepped onto the transport to take me from Ketchikan to the plane landing, I am immediately hit with a mist from the water and an overwhelming sinking feeling in the pit of my stomach. The confused sadness, if you will, was still present as I waved good-bye to Braiden. He stood on the dock, all alone. It's odd, but I could almost feel that he was having the same internal emotional upheaval I was having, both of us feeling insecure, as to when, if ever we would see each other again.

I wanted to very much believe in that fairy tale magic. Those great endings to romance novels or cinema flicks, but I was always a bigger fan of horror films so what does that say about me? He could still be on that next ferry ride or next flight out of here. He could come after me and profess that hc can't live without me. Behind us the mansion would be burning and gunfire and violins would be part of the distant far off noises. My long flowing hair would be blowing in the wind and him in his black velvet jacket with the frilly white shirt. I can dream can't I? I do have that right, being an American and all. Who was I kidding? This is the twentieth century, I am wearing a flannel shirt for crying out loud and I cut all my hair off.

Let's also not forget that Braiden was just too sexy for his own good. Much like I imagine Jim Morrison must have been in his early days. Bray, possessed the makings of a frustrated rock star, mountain man and eternal teenager all rolled into the same being.

Braiden and I were too much alike in our personalities, we had no grounding, and we were both dreamers looking to the other for guidance. He once told me that he believed we each needed a mate stronger than ourselves. I am not sure if he was correct in that, as there is always something to be said for two emotionally charged beings and the wonderful things they create when they bond. I felt it was his way of saying we were co dependent or some kind of enablers to each other's bad habits.

We had fantastic conversations and he is the one who brought otherworldly thinking into my life. He gave me the other side of the coin. He coaxed me to go just that much further in my thoughts. He prodded me into thinking beyond the visible and expanding my mind.

The times we shared will always be with me no matter what the time ahead brings me .I will find comfort in the these memories. The man has style, grace, and beauty that transcends all the outside that he has to offer. The sex was incredible, but I have to say I think maybe youth has the most to do with it. The first times you discover your lover's body, and exploration has to do with most of the excitement.

I feel the main reason our relationship did not make it was that it collapsed under its own pressure, like a black hole in space that only the universe had knowledge of.